A Thief In the
African Night

A Thief In The African Night: The Conflicts of Change

A Peace Corps Writers Book — an imprint of Peace Corps Worldwide

Copyright © 2020 by Joe Miano
All rights reserved.

Printed in the United States of America by
Peace Corps Writers of Oakland, California.

For more information, contact peacecorpsworldwide@gmail.com.

Peace Corps Writers and the Peace Corps Writers colophon are
trademarks of PeaceCorpsWorldwide.org

ISBN: 9781950444151
Library of Congress Control Number: 2020923238

First Peace Corps Writers Edition, August 2020

Cover and Interior Design: Dania Zafar

A Thief In the African Night

THE CONFLICTS OF CHANGE

JOE MIANO

A PEACE CORPS WRITERS BOOK

This book is dedicated to
Ruth
The love of my life,
Whose encouragement and help,
In editing and discussion,
Helped me immensely.

CONTENTS

African Dawn

The African dawn is cold and damp
And comes like a thief in the night
Removing the black and the coldness
And bringing magnificent light!

He is met at the door by the songbirds,
Who quickly spread the alarm.
And by the gazelle and the Tommy,
Whose hooves kick up the dust and the calm.

As he comes he removes the dampness,
And the black clouds all disappear
As he shows his head in his chariot
Of gold-red, yellow-orange, and amber.

So suddenly has the thief come upon us
That the darkness is a memory of old,
And the fear and the chill and the blackness,
All vanish with the chariot of gold!

INTRODUCTION

Three men were born in the dawn of a new Africa. One was born on the plains of the Great Rift Valley near Lake Elmenteita, one on the eastern slopes of Mt. Kenya south of present Meru town, and one not far from the future capital and metropolis, Nairobi.

Each was born into a world of cows, subsistent farms, and wild beasts, but their world would soon change forever with the coming of hunters, explorers, missionaries, and colonizers, and they three would find their neat, small worlds grow and interconnect.

As the sun turns that cool dawn into torrid day, so three men, blinded by the magnificent light of dawn, were unaware that their freedom was gradually being eaten away. That their struggle to adapt only led to more servitude for themselves and their people.

What is this clattering beast charging into the tranquility of centuries long traditions? How does this change these three men's lives? How does this fast moving, chaotic activity bring them to a new world view? How does it open their minds to a dream and a plan for dignity and equality?

BOOK I

THE SAFARI BEGINS

CHAPTER 1

LAIKISAT THE ELDER
(Late 1880s)

T he plains were blessed with rain. This year *Ngai* (God) had smiled on his people and from Poko to Kamumba, from Harisa to Taringo the grass was high, the cows fat with milk, the game abundant, and the hives filled with honey. Neither Laikisat nor any of the elders could remember a time like this in all their years. Not since his first born, Laninyat, entered the world had people been so prosperous. Not since the white father came with his sisters had there been so much game. No, not since the first white man was seen in Arlal did Laikisat remember a time like this!

And in this year when the river Lal flowed and did not stop, Laninyat's wife, Lorret, had conceived. In four moons Laikisat would see himself reborn, for the first-born male of the last son takes the namesake of his grandfather. In him, Laikisat would live on. Already his eyes were dimming – but only if he could live to see his grandsons, would he close his eyes happily. He then could eat his goat and drink his cup of milk and blood knowing he would have someone to remember his soul and his deeds and he could join the spirits of his ancestors. Laikisat prayed that he would live to see this day.

And this day came in four moons and five days. Lorrett opened and the earth laughed with sunshine and with the smell of sweet nectar. A new child, a new spirit, the most precious gift of the Maker, gave its first cry.

Laikisat danced that day! He had not danced since the circumcision of his son years before. But now, not even his crippled leg could keep him still. Laikisat danced! He danced the dance that only an old man could dance. A dance which showed the village his whole life - a dance more beautiful than a bird, more agile than a gazelle, more meaningful than any in the small village could remember. On that night Laikisat's spirit danced, his soul leaped upward like a gazelle leaps for her young.

But as the moon grew old, Laikisat's eyes dimmed. His spirit faded like the moon faded. One night he was full, and in but a few days, empty. But the moon always returns. Laikisat died but was born again.

CHAPTER 2

KAHARA, GICHURU'S FATHER (1880-1906)

T he settlement was forever expanding. Though much of the territory remained as it was before the white man set foot on this great continent, the town was taking on the façade of a colonial outpost. Business was better than ever, what with precious stones, furs and skins, ivory and gold for export, and bands of hunters arriving each day. Also, more settlers were heading for the empty highlands north and west of the capital. This was the time for men to make money and grow fat. There were *Bwana Wakubwa* (Important Men) everywhere – white, black, and brown. Tourism also was surging.

All pointed to a bright future for the town, which 15 years ago was nothing but a sun-drenched plain teaming with game. There had only been a trading center, Ngongo Bagas, now Dagoretti, that was frequented by the Swahili caravans. But ever since the railroad was completed people were arriving and setting up *mabati* (corrugated iron) and wooden buildings along the rails and toward the hills.

They were setting up *dukas* (small shops) and outfitting for hunting safaris. Each day there was something new. Besides whites many East Indians had helped with the railroad and now were setting up dukas of their own.

But before the arrival of the great mechanical Iron Rhino, it was a peaceful place, especially toward the forest and in the regions north toward *Kirinyaga* (Mt. Kenya). The great white mountain, *Kirinyaga*, provided the tribe with all they needed. The volcanic soil was rich and the mountain streams abundant with fresh clean water. The Gikuyu lived in the areas east and south of *Kirinyaga* for countless generations before the white settlers arrived. They built their huts and *shambas* (farm plots) on the verdant foothills and forests above the high plain which the Maasai called *Enkare Nyrobi* (cool water). It was a swampy place. Just above was *Ngongo Bagas*, the marketplace where caravans and traders stopped.

Their homeland was protected to the west by the almost 9000-foot escarpment which fell to the Rift Valley floor below. To the north loomed the great white head of *Kirinyaga* (Mt. Kenya), the home of *Ngai*, their creator and protector. This fine temperate land provided a rich harvest of crops and a place for grazing their goats and cattle. The thick forest provided bamboo and wood for fires and building. It was the ideal place given to them by *Ngai*.

Long ago *Ngai* had promised the man Gikuyu the rich land below *Kirinyaga* and had given him a wife, Mumbi, the Creator and Molder. Together they had nine daughters and provided them husbands whom the daughters ruled until the men planned a coup and took control. The tribe grew to populate and rule the region. This, their land, flowed through their ancestors' blood to them. In this land, held communally by the entire tribe, their ancestors rested in peace and their spirts guided them and spoke to their prophets near the sacred groves and especially the giant fig tree. *Ngai* protected them looking down from the white mountain above them. He was the supreme black god of kindness. The world had its order.

Kahara was a strong Gikuyu who lived northeast of Ngongo, close to the forest. He had many cows and had been a brave warrior. He was very respected. He had seen many caravans and as a very young man he remembered his grandfather telling him about two white men who arrived with a great number of porters. The caravan consisted of Swahili, Kamba, and Arab men. But the two white men seemed to be in charge. They were searching for the great White Mountain which the Gikuyu knew as Kirinyaga. They did not linger long but continued their quest. A few others passed by at other times to hunt and some were holy men, but they did not stay. Still other caravans came to trade and take slaves from other tribes who lived south and west.

Kahara knew Kiswahili, the coastal and trade language. He insisted that Gichuru, his son, learn it as well as the tongues of the other tribes in the area. This would add to his ability to trade and deal with changing times. Kahara learned much from the men in the caravans. He knew this would make him useful to the whites since he heard that many were getting closer. Already rumors of white holy men approaching were filling the air. They already had found outposts in Ukambani.

One day the Gikuyu heard that a caravan with whites was approaching Dagoretti. The Council of Elders met and decided they would need to speak to them to find out more. This Council consisted of all the clans of Gikuyu who resided in a large region in the hills surrounding the papyrus swamp and stretching toward Ngongo. They selected Kahara to speak to the whites and interpret since his command of Kiswahili was excellent.

One day two white men and a number of armed Africans approached one of the elders. Kahara was called and told that they wanted the Council to meet so that they could speak to all about the great Queen Victoria. The next day the group assembled near the forest. Sir Frederick Jackson and James Martin spoke to them as Kahara interpreted. They were told of something called the Imperial British East African Company. It wished to trade with the clans and surrounding tribes. They needed to agree that they would be safe to do so and that in return the Queen would provide protection. When they asked what protection was needed, Jackson told them that there were many other bad Europeans who wanted their land and that there were also Arab slave lords. The Tribal Council told Jackson that they needed time to discuss. He would be called back when a decision was reached.

According the custom, the Council would sit eat and drink honey beer until a consensus was reached. Finally, they decided that they would agree so that they could study these men to find what they really wanted. Kahara was to speak with them and be the Council's spy. He agreed.

The Council called the white men back. These men told the elders that the agreement was called a treaty and that the elders must put a symbol on some paper. The number on the paper was 1889. When the elders asked, they were told whites number the years. They thought this was another strange custom, for the Gikuyu label time using warrior Age-sets. There were many clicking tongues among the gathered elders and warriors, but they signed. And, so, Britain came to the Gikuyu.

For a time, it was quiet. The white caravan went southeast. Years passed. A few caravans came and went. A few hunters passed through. But one day, as Kahara and his age mates sat on a high hill admiring their herds and watching the women in the field, they noticed a great commotion in the distance. Hundreds of men feverishly working. They waited and as the workers got closer, they saw that not all were white; some were brown, some, turbaned, some were Africans of different tribes. They were building a strange road with iron pieces. Others were approaching on horseback and mules. They were carrying supplies and placing them near the papyrus swamp of *Enkare Nyrobi*. In a few days they heard a great sound which shook the ground. A great Iron Rhino, moving stealthily like a prowling cheetah, approached on the new road. Later the white people called this a "locomotive."

But now, to Kahara and the others, it was a very strange beast. It carried many people. Day after day they watched as the Rhino left at night and returned each morning carrying more and more whites, East Indians, and supplies. Near the swamp they added to the few wooden shacks that were already there. The Rhino road came closer, past Kahara's valley and continued up the hills toward the escarpment to vanish in the distance.

Kahara wondered what would happen as it approached the Great Rift. Would it stop? The escarpment at places rose nearly nine-thousand feet above the valley! Would they build a staircase?

Day after day Kahara noticed more and more wood

and mabati (corrugated iron) huts springing up close to the Iron Rhino station. The structures were only about a one-hour walk from his home. They were sprouting faster than the weeds after the rain. Men and women were busy hurrying to and fro, and they now had horses and wagons. He had never seen such busyness. The Rhino carried men and women in its belly and deposited them near the swamp. The white women were very odd looking - too many clothes for the heat. They had long clothing with large headgear and carried sticks with *maridadi* (pretty) cloth roofs to shield themselves from the sun. It was as if he were dreaming. What did they want? Would they take his cows? His children?

He had seen many things in his life and was able to survive - the drought, the flood, disease. His ancestors, *Ngai*, and the witchmen had protected him and his family. He had always followed the old ways. Now Kahara was wondering if there was a growing plot. In particular, he feared it was the working of the Red God of his mortal enemies, the Maasai. He had not seen the white cloud of *Ngai* on *Kirinyaga* (Mt. Kenya) for some time! Was this an omen? Was the world he had known turning inside out?

The Warrior

The walk of the warrior is a noble gait
A springing step at a galloping rate.
The body of the warrior moves in a dancing rhythm
Like the beat of the heart in nature's bosom.

The dress of the warrior is a fire-sheet
Gleaming in the sun of the noon-day heat.
The pride of the warrior in silhouetted light
Is that of a pharaoh walking in might!

CHAPTER 3

LAIKISAT (1890)

"Oh how still the African night can be! And how many stars in the sky!" Laikisat wondered to himself. They were more than all the cows of his clan, the Buru. The Buru were part of the Maasai, a people that filled the plains from north to south– the whole world as far as Laikisat knew. Laikisat in all his fourteen long rains had never been to a land where there were not Maasai.

We are a strong, noble, proud people, he thought. *Someday I too will be a great warrior like my cousin, Lorran. He is a handsome sight painted red like the cow blood that they drank for strength.* His cousin could even fight a *simba* (lion) with his spear and *rungu* (wooden mace); nor did he fear any man. He had also told Laikisat of their grandfather whose spirit Laikisat carries. Lorran repeated his clan's history for Laikisat, just as his grandfather had done for Loran, himself.

"Laikisat, you should know how we came to this place on the plains. Grandfather and the *Wazee* (Elders) had great wisdom and he wished you should know our proud story. We have been here for quite some time, but we are wanderers, always in search of better pastures for our cows and for place where we can raid. We are the bravest warriors in all these lands.

Long ago our *Wazee* say we lived far to the north west where there is a great river. It flows north and becomes very large through a great desert. As the land became drier, we followed it south toward some great lake waters, and then to this valley. The highlands surrounding were welcoming to our cattle in the dry seasons. These lands were vacant and vast. We found a few other nomads, like the Cushites, whom we befriended and intermarried. And so now we are the undisputed lords of this land."

Laikisat listened with great interest. "I have never heard of this before. There are great rivers? Large lakes?"

"Yes," replied Lorran, "when you become a warrior you will see one large one in the northern desert. It is in the land of the Turkana. And to the south you will find the great mountains covered in white!"

"White? What makes them white?"

"These are places you will discover once you become a *murran* (warrior). I tell you these things because it is your heritage. You must know this to feel you belong to the land and to your people. You will learn more as time permits.

Lorran continued to tell him of his grandfather's life and how brave and good grandfather was. Lorran told him that he did not fear others, even the Gikuyu to the east. Laikisat could not comprehend a different people. Perhaps one day he would see a Gikuyu warrior himself!

But for now, Laikisat sat and thought, played and sparred with his good friend, Letegall. They watched their fathers' cows together, still fat after the heavy rains, even though the short rains had not yet begun. The rains were late, and the grass was just beginning to brown.

Letegall, Laikisat's friend and age mate, thought out loud, "If the rains do not come soon, the cows will no longer give milk."

"I can never remember a time without milk" said Laikisat.

"My mother said that before we were born, there were years when there was no milk and the land turned to dust. These were the times of the great migrations to the hills. They were hard times and there were wars with others who also were starving," remembered Letegall.

But if the rains fail in these times, will we too have to migrate? Thought Laikisat.

Migration? A way to see different places. Laikisat imagined it would not be so bad after all. He had heard about mountains and forests from his cousin. Places far and difficult to get to. So far! No Buru even lived there. Lorran had told him that he had heard from others that there was even a huge village, with many more people than all the Buru. The people were white, black, and brown. A place where a white man was the leader with his own warriors for protection.

Laikisat was filled with wonder. *How I dream of a great safari to such a place! If I could only leave our cows! Maybe once I become a warrior.*

After all, Laikisat was almost a man. He came from a race of wanderers. Now he knew that his tribe had journeyed far from the north following a great river and down many escarpments. They had conquered many peoples and moved on to the fertile grass plains and uplands. After all, this was in his blood -- to move, see new places, increase his herds, and produce children.

Yes, how good to be free thought Laikisat, *I will be free to go where I please someday. After my circumcision, then I will wander to see new places. Oh, to be free! But right now, I will settle down to watch my father's goats and cows until that day. The day will come when I will leave this work to my younger brothers. Yes, that will be a happy day – that will be the day of my freedom!*

CHAPTER 4

GICHURU'S BIRTH
(late 1880s - 1903)

O ne dreary year the rains were heavier and longer than anyone could remember. Each day was cloud covered and raw. It was mid-season when the grass was as high as a man's hips, the sausage flies swarmed, and the forest trails were slippery with mud. It was then that Kahara's first wife delivered a healthy son, Gichuru.

Kahara knew Gichuru would become an important man when he grew up. He knew that there would be few Africans who would have Gichuru's opportunities and connections. He knew that he must prepare his son for the changing world. Kahara had heard that the white men and the white god people were already by the great saltwater and in Kamba land. He realized that it was important to be open to change for the good of Gichuru and the rest of his sons.

It was later known to Kahara that the birth of his son was in the same year Sir William Mackinnon[1] became Chairman of the IBEAC, the Imperial British East Africa Company, in Mombasa.

Gichuru grew into a healthy and intelligent young man who was eager to learn from the elders and older boys in the foothills above *Enkare Nyrobi*. From his family *shamba* (fields), each day the young Gichuru could watch the Iron Rhino approaching the growing town as he drank the chai which his mother had prepared. Up here on the hills, the air was quiet and peaceful. He and his family sat like birds observing the growing busyness below.

The Rhino made two trips each week from the coast and went on toward the Great Lake Nyanza (*Nam Lolwe*), but which now bore the name of Queen Victoria. It still amazed Gichuru to see the Iron Rhino rising from the plains heading west.

He had learned all about it in his school at the Scottish Mission in Kabete. He was grateful to the missionaries for teaching him to read and write, but also to better understand the white men's strange ways.

One day when he was still a boy, he and his father noticed smoke and flames in the plain below. The whole of Nairobi was burning! The old wooden houses and dukas (stores) were burning to the ground! When he got closer to inquire, he was told that the Bwana Daktari had ordered the whole town burnt because there had been a plague. Gichuru thought that this was another example of strange white witch doctor medicine. He was trying to understand, but this was beyond his comprehension. Perhaps it was a way to rid the place of the evil spirits that lived in the swamp.[2]

But now, since it was nearing the end of the dry season, Gichuru would prepare to return to the mission school at Kabete. Maybe there he would gain some insight into the strange ways of these *Wazungu* (Europeans)!

CHAPTER 5

NJAGE'S BIRTH (1890s)

One group of Bantu, the Meru, settled on the northern and eastern slopes of the great mountain, *Kirimara* (Mt. Kenya). They had come in waves and settled in different regions; each region divided by a crystalline river flowing from the glaciers.

The rains in Muthambe, Meru, had been especially long and abundant following the few years of drought. The people were overjoyed that they finally would have substantial crops. The ridges were green and plush. Kithingi was hoping the floods would subside soon so that the women could begin planting. The bananas had begun to flower as the sun showed its face more each day. Hopefully the rain would cease so that the young fruit would ripen and not mold. Kithingi's wife was about to deliver and he hoped it would be soon. She too was needed to work preparing the fields. His mother and sister were already there.

Kithingi was hoping for a son to carry on the warrior tradition. He already had two young girls, but he needed a male to help with the family as he aged. He came from a long line of brave warriors who became respected elders. He followed his ancestors back many age sets to the time of Lawi, his first known ancestor, for whom many songs were sung during festivities. He was proud of his heritage.

Kithingi enjoyed sitting with the old men by the fire and listening to their recounting the past. As night fell Kithingi went to visit his grandfather, Sabari. Sabari was an ancient soul, probably the eldest in the clan. You could tell that he had been a tall and slender man. Now he had gnarled fingers and bent legs. He walked with a bent back, but his mind was sharp.

"*Muga* (greetings), Sabari! Shall we sit and speak for a while?"

"Come, Kithingi, it is good to see you! You will be a father again very soon. Sit here."

After exchanging some news, the spirit seemed to take hold of Sabari, and he began to recite: "*Murungu* (God) has always been the protector of our tribe. Our clan and our family have done great things. We live close to Him. We see his cloud over *Kirimara* (Mt. Kenya) and he speaks to us. We are descended from the mighty Lawi, but before him there were others, far in the past. Our ancestors tell us that the Bantu travelled great distances. They started in the far west, beyond the great lakes and the Rift, and arrived at the great salt sea to the protected place, Mbwaa. There, surrounded by the waters they were very safe and lived for many years. These places were rich with the bounty of the sea. The coconut palm provided them with food and drink, but also materials for boats, clothing, building materials and myriad other useful items.

"*Murungu* smiled upon them and they prospered until evil entered their world from the sea. From afar evil came and they decided to flee. They wandered for many years. They traveled along the rivers over savannah and desert until they reached the foothills of *Kirimara*. Lawi and the others of the Mukuruma Age-Set were the first to arrive on the foothills of the Mountain. He and his fellow warriors fought off the few Dorobo and established us here. Grandson, always remember your ancestors and from where you have come. Tell your children. Do not let them forget. Our spirits only live when all of us remember. Remember!"

"Sabari, I deeply respect you and your knowledge. I always learn when you speak. I will return and bring my children to you so your spirit can reside with them also, as you do with me. Rest now and stay strong. *Asante!* (Thank you) I will go now."

"*Murungu* protect you, my grandson. Soon a new spirit will enter the world and we will be blest."

Kithingi left and retired for the night and slept soundly. He had gained more knowledge of his ancestors and was filled with hope about the child that soon would be his.

After a few days the sky began to clear in the morning to the deepest blue. *Kirimara* (Mt. Kenya) reared its head and could be seen clearly from the top of the ridge. The white hair of God circled the peak, whiter than ever they could remember. The air smelled of sweetness and the women could be heard singing and ululating near his wife's hut. He ran to see what the excitement was all about. His mother stood at the entrance holding up a newborn. "*Ni nthaka!* - It is a son!" Kithingi was filled with joy and thanked *Murungu* (God) for his good fortune. He had fulfilled his ancestors wishes. They now lived yet for another generation and he knew that Njage would grow and make him and the Meru people proud.

Lawi's branch of the clan was always a powerhouse in Lower Muthambe. As Njage grew, people saw that he inherited the tallness and the strong body of his legendary ancestor. As a child he was the quickest to climb up and down the ridges and was full of adventure. He loved to explore the lower valleys and up to the edge of the forest. He was quick of mind and had begun to pick up Kiswahili at an early age. He was born in a time of plenty, so his diet helped him achieve the physique of a warrior at an early age. He was destined to achieve great things.

CHAPTER 6

GICHURU'S EDUCATION AND APPOINTMENT
(late 1890s, early 1900s)

Final examinations were close at hand and Gichuru was studying feverishly. He felt well prepared by the Scottish missionaries in Kabete. When Gichuru was still a young boy, Kahara learned about the White God People in Kabete who were teaching children to read and write like the Swahili people. They also were teaching them *Kingereza* (English), the speech of the English King. Kahara had used his influence with the White Chief in Nairobi to see that his eldest son would board at the mission school and work to earn his keep. Kahara knew how useful his knowledge of Kiswahili was to him. Gichuru learning *Kingereza* (English) would ensure more protection and wealth for his family. So, Kahara had sent Gichuru away to learn from the White God People.

Now Kahara was starting to see his decision was for the better. Gichuru had not only learned the White Man's God Book, but also to read, write, and calculate. He also learned of white customs and history. The exam he took was prepared at Cambridge. And even though he had not been to that damp island called Great Britain, he felt that he had enough knowledge to succeed. He was one of the first Africans to earn a diploma. He had put his mind to work like a pestle to the grinding stone! But it was hard to concentrate when so much was going on and changing near him. Gichuru knew that this would help him adjust to the fast-changing world of the whites. Kahara was very proud of Gichuru's success.

Now Gichuru was growing into a handsome strong young man. Though of average height for a Gikuyu, he had strong arms and felt ready to enter the warrior Age-Set. Things were different than in even in his father's time. Though he would go through the initiation into manhood, he would no longer be allowed to carry weapons. This is one of the first prohibitions laid down by the British. However, he felt like his education was serving him as protection and he also had many friends among his fellow initiates.

One day not long after leaving Kabete, Gichuru entered the new town of Nairobi on foot. Since the fire had destroyed the Nairobi he had remembered as a child, the place had been rebuilt quickly and was a lot cleaner and ordered. He walked down First Station Road, the new road that went all the way to the Iron Rhino station! Soon its name would change to Government Road. The other main road was called Victoria Street which ran parallel to Government Road. By now he was comfortable with the whites. The whites actually liked this place better than Mombasa, for they had just moved the capital here. A new large house was being built for the Governor not far from his father's *shamba* (field).

Gichuru had been summoned to the Government House where he was to meet with Sir James Sadler, the new Governor. When he entered, he saw a few younger Gikuyu from other clans. They all spoke excellent Kiswahili, but only Gichuru knew *Kingereza* (English). The Governor told them they would be called chiefs and that he, Gichuru, would be the chief of chiefs among them. They presented each of them with a black blanket. They were all a bit confused. The Gikuyu people did not have this "chief" title in their tradition.

He was taken aside and given the right to build a small hut on the edge of the forest where he could farm and keep goats and cows, not far from Kahara. They also gave him some rupees to buy materials. The British remembered that Gichuru's father, Kahara, had helped them translate and talk to the elders. They appreciated his family's help. He found that a chief's duty was to carry back instructions from the Governor and the King to the Gikuyu elders.

Gichuru was certainly pleased at the good words of the Governor and for his gifts. However, he was confused by what was meant by "chief" and "chief of chiefs". It seemed that they wanted him to be a go-between for the Governor and the elders, who together with the tribal prophets ruled his people. As he walked up the hills to his father's shamba, he began to wonder to himself, *how would the elders react to hearing what he was instructed to tell them? I must always be respectful and not offend!* For the Gikuyu, it was the elders who made the laws and executed them. He, as a young man, was of the warrior class. However, warriors could no longer raid or plunder. They were forbidden by the British to practice warrior activities. The British had confiscated all their weapons and forbade all such activities.

On his walk to the hills, Gichuru's mind was filled with many thoughts and images. His father promised to prepare a bride price for him so that when he grew old enough to pass out of the Warrior Age-Set, he could marry Wanjiku.

She was a girl from his uncle's village far across the Rift Valley in Molo. His uncle, Njoroge, was a trader and had settled in this far off place. Wanjiku's family also lived in Molo. Her father and Njoroge worked together. Gichuru hoped his father would take him to Molo someday soon to meet her. Now, however, he wondered about his duties and what exactly the Governor wanted him to do. Would this conflict with his tribal rites of passage that were required to enter marriage?

It was not until much later that Gichuru realized what "chief" meant to the British.

CHAPTER 7

LAIKISAT: MANHOOD
(Late 1800's)

F inally, the day arrived! Laikisat had been prepared. The night before the elders had prepared the boys for their initiation into manhood. The young men had danced the dance of the warriors. Their chests and legs were painted with ochre and they spent many hours having their hair plated. The age group made a magnificent spectacle. Toned lean bodies, without a trace of fat. They jumped high like gazelles for many hours dancing and singing in a bewitching chant, while a constant hum emanated from deep within their chests that vibrated everyone's bones.

The young girls had also danced. Covered in colorful beads, bare-chested, with huge earrings and beaded headdresses in red, green, black and white. They circled the young men who jumped and pranced, moving toward and away in a sexual, enticing, rhythm – never touching, but filled with teenage desire.

Early before the dawn the boys were cleansed with

a shower of cold water. All were marched away by the appointed elders to the secluded, secret *manyatta* (Maasai compound) especially built for the ceremony. The ceremony would transform the young boys into men, into Il-murran, warriors. They would remain secluded until they healed and emerged to replace the current warriors who would pass to the next stage – family men who would take wives and raise the next generation of warriors and women. This completes the cycle of life and keeps traditions alive. The oldest men in the village would remind the young of these traditions, where they came from and what was expected of each Age-Set. So, it has been, and so will it continue.

Laikisat thought about the pain he would endure but knew that only through pain would he and his age mates be made strong. He knew that in a few weeks he would emerge as someone who could lead, as someone who would kill his lion, and be a warrior like his father, and grandfather. They both had been respected and his grandfather had been an enlightened and intelligent elder. His grandfather led his people through good and bad times as they wandered the plains, moving with the rains from the lowlands to the uplands. Their land was a great, beautiful, bounteous land.

The pain of circumcision certainly was great, but he did not flinch. The ordeal was over before he knew it. To have cried out would have declared to his people that he was not a man. It would bring disgrace upon him, his family, and, especially, his ancestors. After the ceremony he would dress in black until he was well. During the months of healing he and his age group would be secluded in this manyatta far from the tribe.

That night after the circumcision Laikisat fell into a very deep sleep. Now his ancestors visited him in his dreams.

The next day he did not recall all of the visitations, except that of his grandfather, Laikisat, whom he had been named after. The new warrior heard a distant voice: "Laikisat, Laikisat, I am your grandfather. I knew you but you never knew me! You will know me because I will hold you close!"

He reminded the new *Il-murran* (warrior) of Engai, their god. He was told to remember what he had been taught. Engai took his full form only after dividing the sky and earth by his first creation, Ol Doinyo Lengai, god's mountain.

"Remember, remember," said his grandfather "how *Engai Narok*, the Black God, the benevolent side of god, gave us Maasai all the cattle in the world. Now as Il-murran you may raid and capture all cattle from other peoples, for cows are all ours. Also remember to beware of the other side of god, *Engai Na-nyokie*, the vengeful red god. He brings us problems and suffering; but there is always prayer, libations, and the Laibons who can heal, divine and prophecy, and make rain or give us victory! Remember my son, remember me, and remember your ancestors. I am watching over you!"

Laikisat felt the presence of his grandfather even though he had never known him. He felt as if he had slept cradled in his arms with the vision of the Male-Female Engai smiling down on them both from a white cloud circling Ol Doinyo Lengai. He would never forget this first night of his manhood.

Now, awake, Laikisat thought of all he had already seen. Strange and new things — groups of white-red hunters setting up camp, bringing houses made of cloth, strange four-legged wooden objects, and seats. They would cover these objects with a cloth and have other Africans place food and drink on it, and the whites would sit and consume for many hours at dawn, noon, and even after dusk by the fire. Africans with strange red hats and white robes would stand like slaves pouring drinks, serving food, and pampering them. It so disgusted Laikisat. Then the white-red people would ride horses or camels into the bush to kill lion, or zebra, or elephant. Laikisat could understand the lion and the zebra. He could not understand the butchering of the elephant. They would leave the meat of the magnificent beast to rot, while only removing the ivory. His people rarely killed elephant, but it was in times of great drought when little else was available or if they posed a danger to a *manyatta*. It would feed a village for many months. Then and only then, would they remove the ivory to make implements or jewelry. "But these men," reasoned Laikisat, "were very greedy men."

He wanted to know more about these men, for only knowing the enemy could one control one's destiny and defeat them. Were these men sent by *Engai Na-nyokie*, the Red God ? So much unknown!

CHAPTER 8

FIRST SIGHTING (early 1900)

The tribal warriors were the first to explore new territory. M'Mkira was one such Ameru who explored the higher reaches of *Kirimara* (Mt. Kenya) soon after they arrived on the mountain's foothills. He was a descendent of the legendary brave Lawi after whom many songs were sung. M'Mkira and his fellow warriors chased out whom they called the small people, who hunted and gathered. They then built their huts, and when they passed into adulthood, brought their wives and established permanent homesteads. Once the newer age group was circumcised, M'Mkira's generation produced many healthy children like Ikiara. Ikiara's great, great, grandson, Njage, was hunting gazelle one day in the lowlands. Suddenly he saw a warrior with red-colored shoulders, long plaited hair and red-beaded necklaces, who was covered only with a small ochre loin cloth. He had never seen this kind of warrior. So much taller, leaner, muscular than his people. He walked alone with great determination with a spring in his step. The encounter would change both Njage and the ocher-covered warrior forever.

Njage was a skilled Ameru hunter. He saw the gazelle on the lower plains near Thoraka. It was the dry season. The sorghum supply was dwindling. Only a few root crops remained in their storehouses. The people were waiting for *Murungu* (God) to open the sky. Now as he aimed his arrow at the gazelle, Njage saw that the other warrior was also looking to strike with his spear. Instantly, Njage was ready. He let his arrow fly! It was a clean kill right at the neck. The other warrior put his spear down and approached.

"*Hujambo, mimi niitwa* Laikisat. I am called Laikisat."

"Stop! Do not approach any closer. *Mimi, ni* Njage."

"You are from a mountain tribe?"

"Yes, I am Ameru."

"And I, Maasai. It is good we both speak Kiswahili. You have made a good kill."

"Yes. It was clean. But we Meru have been warned about you Maasai! Are you and your fellow warriors here to raid our cattle? Beware if that is your intention. If I call, fifty warriors will be here in minutes!"

"No, Njage. I am alone. I have been on raids and killed my lion. But this journey is to see the great mountain. I have seen it from afar since I was a child. Now I wish for adventure. To quell my curiosity about new places. I have been told about the Meru and the Gikuyu from the elders and have been warned. I wish no harm to you."

"I am hunting because our people, the Meru, have little food because of the dry season. We usually live on what we plant, but now we need to augment our supplies with meat."

"I also have seen many changes on the plains. More white hunters come each day. They even bring their women. I wish to learn from the mountain people if they have seen similar things."

"I have not here in Meru, but our elders have seen white men long ago. Our elders believe they will also come here in a few moons. Stay here with me, Laikisat, and let us share this kill. Later we can hunt together, if you are not opposed."

"*Asante*. Let us hunt together and then eat and talk. The world is changing quickly, and we need to share what we know and how to deal with this new world."

And so, this very unusual partnership was forged between the two men who would normally be at each other's throats. Why was this different? Only *Murungu, Engai* could know.

At the end of the hunt they sat by a fire and discussed about their lives and what they had seen. Laikisat told Njage of the white hunters and the White God People whom he had seen near Machakos. This was the first Njage had heard of white people since the tales the elders had told him of those who searched for *Kirimara* (Mt. Kenya) long ago. He would report back to the elders as soon as he went home. They agreed to meet again to share more news and maybe to trade. They each returned to their people and shared a different view of life and the new dangers and possibilities that had been born that day.

CHAPTER 9

GICHURU AND THE
BRITISH KODI (TAX) (1901)

G ichuru had been trading with the British for a while. His compound near the forest had grown and his *shamba* (field) was productive. The land now belonged to him the way the whites owned theirs. He had a paper that said so. Though he trusted the paper he wondered if it would be respected if new British Commissioners or rulers took charge. The land was part of his reward for assisting the British in translating and bringing his people to follow the law. No longer was land in this region near the capital owned in common by the tribe as in their homelands. Since this land was vacant when the whites arrived, they took ownership, and no one knew to question it. Gichuru had learned from them. He even had planted some coffee trees. They were now finally starting to bear fruit and he was getting a good price. Being chief was paying off. However, he still felt subservient. He usually tried pushing this to the back of his mind, but there were days when he wished there was more certainty about the future. Should he place so much trust in the British? He felt compromised. Was he giving up his tribal values to accommodate the new rulers?

On the other hand, Gichuru felt important, especially when he was called by the Commissioner or other officials to help translate, or to tell the elders the new policies. He enjoyed being a government clerk because he could help many people fill in the new forms required for many things. The elders, especially, were not always pleased with the new rules the whites were spewing, but the younger men accepted more of them without complaining, since they knew no other way. But no part of this was his fault, he reasoned. He was just the go-between and he could not help it if it was to his advantage.

For the most part the Gikuyu agreed - agreed to not let the Witchmen put curses or mark certain lands with curses, but when they went further into the forest, they still did as they pleased. This was their right and culture for generations. The elders still ruled the traditions of the tribe, they held councils in secret, drank all the honey and millet beer they wished, and gave orders when consensus was reached. This had been their way since any could remember, and they would teach this to the warriors once they progressed into the elder age group. Gichuru noticed that the young did not tell the elders all that was occurring. It was getting more and more difficult to get the young to follow the marriage and conduct rules.

Now it was 1901 and Gichuru was to explain a new British directive to the Council of Elders.

"*Hujambo, Wazee* (Old Ones)! Iko habari ya Bwana Eliot. I have news from Commissioner Eliot," Gichuru began.

"What does he want now? Each time you come you

bring us more news of drought or flood," replied one *Mzee* (old one).

"I am only doing my job. I also feel the heaviness of what I am to tell you."

"On with it. They have made us like old women who must only listen and obey!"

"Eliot has said that now all tribesmen must pay for their protection."

"Protection from what? Wild boars? We already can protect ourselves."

"He says that each hut must pay one rupee, or the equivalent in livestock, or labor."

"What is this *Kodi* (Hut Tax)[3]? We should pay for the huts we and our women have built with our hands on the tribe's land! So now, we must work for them like slaves! This is an outrage! We might be able to pay when there are sufficient rains and prosperity, but what will happen in years of drought or plague?"

Gichuru expected unhappiness but was not prepared for such an outburst. Trying to calm the old man, he said, "I too am not happy with this, but what can we do? I will tell the Bwana that you are not happy. I can only relay your outrage. But you should see this as an extension of our own traditions. We pay cows for marriage and take payment for favors and the removal of curses or disagreements."

The *Mzee* was calmer, but not appeased. "Eliot does not even come to see us. He stays in Mombasa and proclaims edicts! We will meet in Council in private, but I can tell you the others are as angry as I am. I can read their faces."

"Please, *Mzee*, take care! These men are powerful. They have already gone as far as Uganda and beyond. The Iron Rhino has already approached the Rift and goes beyond

Maasai land. They are here to stay. Look how many come each day on the Iron Rhino. Our best plan is to wait and plan. We know the land and the hearts of our people. We must learn from the *Waingereza* (English) so we can fight on their terms. I hear Eliot is forming military bands made up of Somalis and other tribes. They are to carry out his orders and punish those that do not obey. Please listen to me, even though I am no wise *Mzee*. I will take my leave, now. *Kwaheri* (Goodbye)."

"*Kwaheri*, Gichuru. Our dissatisfaction is not with you. You need to keep doing your work and tell us what you can."

So Gichuru left. He felt his heart in his mouth. He liked this part of his job least. What can he do? How could he make life better for his people? What would happen to those who did not pay the *Kodi* (Tax)?

Only *Ngai* (God) knew the answers.

CHAPTER 10

OMARI (late 1600, early 1700)

It has been called the Dark Continent for its dark-skinned people and because to Europe much was unknown. The Africans, however, knew this great landmass from the beginning of time. The East African coast was another matter. It has been host to many visitors from ancient times: most recently Europeans and Arabs, but Egyptians, Romans, Greeks, Chinese, Persians, and South Indians from long ago. Arabs and Persians had visited to trade with the Bantu and eventually started to intermarry and start settlements. The trade was for ebony, ivory, mangrove, gold, elephants and exotic animals, and, most importantly, slaves.

In the first century BCE, Akinos, a Greek navigator left Egypt and set sail on the Red Sea and down the Coast. There he encountered Bantu speaking people. Their origin was shrouded in the mists of history, but their legends were filled with endless treks from the high center of this continent, following large rivers, past high mountains covered in white, until they reached the great saltwater.

These tribes traded with Akinos. They had supplies of goods that the Greeks and Egyptians desired. The people happily traded these items for beads, metal objects, and coins. As they sailed down the coast, they found similar settlements with similar language and customs.

The people of the region were the Pokomo and the Mijikende. For years nine major Bantu tribes, Duruma, Kambe, Jibana, Kaume, Rabai, Giriama, Dogi, Chonyi, and Ribi, had intermarried and formed strong alliances. They settled along the coast and the islands off the mainland and became prosperous. The vegetation was rich and plentiful, and the sea was full of life. Later Persians and Arabs arrived bringing their culture and language, intermarrying and slowly forming a new language.

From very early times Ancient Greeks, Romans and Arabs visited and left their coins and trinkets. As the ferment brewed on the Arabian Peninsula, with the rising of a Great Prophet and a revolutionary faith, factions and Civil War arose. Refugees began to arrive as early as 613 CE from varied regions – Oman, Yemen, and Persia. All settling among the Bantu. Learning their language and introducing new words. The Arabs called this region the Sahel – the coast. And so, the Mijikende were labeled as Swahili and their enriched language Kiswahili.

Omari was born into this civilization. He had learned navigation on his father's great dhow and had travelled as far as India and Persia on the monsoon. Omari's family had become wealthy. They returned with spices and strange plants in exchange for mangrove, slaves, and gold. But now Omari wished for more adventure. Omari had asked his father, Sharif, to allow him to join the caravan that was venturing far inland. The Swahili had heard from others of the Great White Mountains that rose from the plains where God resided, where there was abundance, and where many different tribes resided. These tribes were selling exotic goods as well as slaves. Omari had always wanted to join a caravan and to see these wonders for himself.

Sharif had appointed Ahmed, a muscular tall Arab with many scars- badges of honor delivered by wild animals and warriors - to lead the caravan. He was always victorious. His band consisted of fifty men and women. The women slave wives would be porters and workers. Other slaves would carry tents and spears. The journey would last many moons as they followed rivers through desert, scrub, savannah, and highlands until they reached the great forest and the mountains. They went also in search of certain plants and trees, which provided medicines and potions. They also desired animal pelts to wear and trade. They searched for ebony, the hardest and most indestructible wood known. But most of all, they wished to acquire slaves.

Once the caravan was almost ready Sharif told Omari he was now old enough to safari inland. Omari was overjoyed that his father was giving him this exciting adventure and honor.

The caravan began its long and arduous journey following the Tana River. They trekked for many days until they finally arrived at a small village on the slopes of a great mountain. The mountain was known by different names by each different tribe. The names described the indescribable majesty! It was known as *Kirimara*, the mountain of white features, *Kirinyaga*, the mountain of white patches, *Ol Doinyo Keri*, the striped mountain, *Kiima Kya Kenia*, the mountain that glitters! This was what the British later named Mount Kenya, as it is known today.

And there in the cool green paradise, there, he saw her: Mahiri! She was young. Her breasts shone in the sunlight, her hips, wide. She would birth many healthy children. But most of all her face had the look of the *Malaika* (angel) that Omari dreamed about when reading the Koran. He decided he must have her. He would give anything for her!

At the appropriate time when the barter started, he approached the Ameru Lawi, who was in charge of the barter. They spent a long time bargaining because she was his daughter and he was a respected man who had been a brave warrior. The bride price was high, and he had to agree that she was not to be taken as a slave wife, but as his first wife, to be respected and not harmed. He could take a cane to her if she disobeyed consistently, but not to draw blood. Lawi and the elders told him that the *Kiama* (male Council of one Age-Set) would dance and place a curse on Omari if he disobeyed. Omari could not believe his good fortune! He was overjoyed at the prospect of marrying Mahiri! He agreed to all terms, including gifting two baskets of coastal rice, two donkeys, gold and silver jewelry, and a fine rug woven near his home in Lamu. He knew his father would be pleased. Even though it was *haram* (forbidden), Omari even agreed to drink from the cup to seal the deal.

Now that the gourd of beer had been passed and the dance, completed, Omari was free to speak to her.

"*Hujambo*, Mahiri. I am your husband, Omari."

She nodded, for she knew that she must obey her father and go with him to a far place where the water was of salt. That was the way of the tribe and the place of women in it. It was the cycle of life. She had looked at Omari, noticed that he was very different from the members of her tribe, but she did not find him displeasing.

"*Jina lako ninani*? (What is your name?)" she asked timidly.

Omari was astounded! She spoke in his language!
"Jina langu ni Omari. (I am called Omari.)" "How do
you know Kiswahili?"

"I speak a little and understand more. My uncle, a trader,
told me I should learn, and he taught me."

"My father is a rich merchant and seaman in Lamu, a
place by the great sea. I will take you there and you will
live in my house."

"I don't understand 'sea.'"

"O, the great saltwater."

"Then it is useless!"

"No, it is full of many fish and provides for many
abundantly. You will see."

"I will do your bidding. I like your face. But please do
not harm me!"

"I have promised to be kind. And I am a believer in
Allah. Many of my fellow men treat slaves and women
disgracefully, but I am not that kind. My father, but mostly
my older brother, are the ones who trade in slaves, and
I must do their bidding. But for me, I wish to leave this
trade as soon as I am older. Even our prophet, Mohammed,
freed his slave and married her!"

"Allah?"

"It is our name for God. You will learn. You must teach
me more of your language. I know "Muga," your greeting,
and a few phrases, but I want to able to converse."

"It is not hard. Many words are similar. We will teach
each other."

"Go prepare your things. We must begin our journey
soon. It is far and takes many moons. We leave in two days.
We follow the rivers until we reach the great sea."

"Come and eat well, for we must fortify ourselves."

CHAPTER 11

GICHURU ASSIGNED TO MERU (1904-06)

Gichuru had studied hard at the mission school in Kabete. He did especially well in languages and mathematics. He was planning on being a trader like his father. The white people treated him well and they gave him honors when he did well. He already knew the languages of the people around Mt. Kenya, as well as *Maa*, the language of the Maasai, and Kiswahili. His English was improving day by day.

He also did his best to fulfill his tribal obligations as a warrior. This was difficult because of British restrictions. The God people also frowned on the tribal ways. So he and his age mates practiced their combat skills secretly in the forest. However, he still was appreciative of the education he was getting at the mission school. Gichuru realized that this would ultimately help his people, the Gikuyu. He had accepted the title of Chief, but so far, he had not been told what would be entailed. That was to change shortly.

One day as he was walking home from school at the

end of his last term, he met his father, Kahara, along the way who told him that he had been to the newly built Government House. The new Governor, Sir James Hayes Sadler, had told Kahara he would like to see Gichuru. They had a new job for the young man.

Though Gichuru enjoyed learning, he was ready for adventure. Arriving at the office, he saw many important white men dressed in uniform. The first to speak was Sir James, who had just arrived on the Iron Rhino.

"Good Day, m'boy!"

"Good Day, Sir," responded Gichuru.

"I hear you have passed your examinations with high honors. You should be congratulated."

"Thank you, Sir!"

"We have a proposition for you from Mr. Edward Butler Horne, who has an assignment for you. He would like you to accompany him to Meru country."

"My father says the Meru are a fierce tribe."

"Yes, but I know you can speak their tongue and can translate well to ours."

"Yes sir, I will try," Gichuru responded in a quiet voice.

"This is Sir Edward Butler Horne. He will be leading the expedition," said Sir James as he introduced the short but muscled young man standing behind him.

"Good day, Gichuru, I need a good man to help me to conquer this area. I also need instruction in their language. I already know Maasai, and some Kikuyu. You will help me." Horne spoke with authority.

"Yes sir. When are you planning to leave?"

"In a week's time. I must assemble one-hundred porters and the King's African Rifles (KAR). We must be prepared. I understand that we must pass through Embu country. I know the Embu are especially wild. I was in the country a few years ago on a previous expedition."

"I think we should first talk with the Embu. They may be fierce, but I believe they will see that cooperation may be to their benefit. Then they may allow us to pass through," Gichuru said, trying to calm Horne's view of the Embu.

"Thank you, Gichuru. I see that we will get on splendidly."

Sadler, speaking from behind his desk as he shuffled papers, looked bored. "Good, good. Gichuru, I will give you authority. I will give you the title of Chief Official Translator. God be with you!"

"Thank you, Sirs. You will not be disappointed. I must also make my father proud."

"Boy, come in the morning so we can talk about the expedition," ordered Horne.

"Yes, Sir."

"Thank you all. Good Day," said Sadler as he rose to open the office door.

"Good day, sirs, you will not be disappointed," Gichuru repeated as he turned to leave Sadler's ornate office.

Gichuru could not believe what had just happened. Not only was he off on an adventure but was given a great honor. He would do his best to show them that he could do an excellent job. He could not wait to share the news with his father, but mostly with the warriors of his age group. Ever since the white men arrived, warriors had not been fighting and their movements were restricted. Now, only he would have an adventure among his age mates. Meru awaited.

GICHURU IN MERU (1907)

H orne had assembled a great retinue of one-
hundred porters and workers, fifty King's African
Rifles (KAR), and a personal Maasai guard chosen
especially for their height and fierceness. They were to
travel east and then north circling Mt. Kenya, establishing
outposts until they reached the northern extent of Meru
country.

Previously another British contingent, including Horne
as one of its members, had tried to subdue the Embu, a tribe
on the southeastern flank of Mt. Kenya. However, once
the Embu saw the powerful shooting sticks of the British,
the clan had scattered into the deep forest and the British
withdrew back to Nairobi. Reports of the firing sticks and
the warriors killed and wounded in the skirmish quickly
spread around the Mountain. The British had no idea how
quickly news travelled in Africa.

Gichuru stayed close to Horne as they began their trek.
The Meru lived on ridges that were the foothills of *Kirima
Kia Maara*. This was their name for Mt. Kenya which
loomed above their huts and farms. *Murungu* (God) resided

there, especially when his white cloud surrounded the mountain. The hills below were covered in lush vegetation. Near their villages the Meru used natural vines to their advantage by weaving them around the trees forming walls so as to be impenetrable to intruders. Their villages were therefore protected on top of each ridge. There were secret gateways known only to the clan where they could move freely from ridge to ridge and this system made it exceptionally easy to defend the villages if breached by invaders.

So, Horne's men travelled up a ridge and down each valley. The work cutting through the brush was difficult. At the bottom of each valley was a fast-flowing stream that originated at the top of Mt. Kenya. Being the dry season, most streams were easily forded, but a few were large. Horne ordered great trees to be felled and vines to be cleared in order to have a clear crossing. Horne had them create bridges with the large trees secured by rope to afford a crossing of the larger streams. This process took longer than he had planned, for the ravines were high and steep, and the valleys deep. He imagined the great increase in difficulty of the journey when the rains came. He was glad it was the dry season.

Butler Horne, an outdoorsman and hunter, was a short man, but strong. He seemed to pick up nicknames wherever he went. He was later nicknamed *Kangangi* (Little Walker) by the Meru. He also knew how to use pomp and drama to his advantage. He had a plan as to how he was going to present himself.

The KAR had been formed a few years before and consisted of men from many tribes and races - Somalis, Arabs, Gikuyu, Kamba, East Indians. Members for a particular expedition were always chosen from tribes different from those whom they were trying to rule or subdue. Everywhere they went the British followed the dictum: Divide and Conquer!

Gichuru waited anxiously for the first encounter with the Meru.

BOOK 2:

COLONIZATION

CHAPTER 13

THE BRITISH (1880-1908)

T he first Europeans to reach the interior were Reverend Johann Kraph and Reverend Johannes Rebmann as agents of the Anglican Church Missionary Society. In 1849 Kraph reached Mt. Kenya. In 1883 Joseph Thompson, a British traveler, was the first European to enter Maasai territory. This led in 1890 to the agreement to divide Maasai Land between Britain and Germany. This began the European control of the peoples of East Africa. Slowly but surely their culture would be attacked, controlled, and removed from most of the people's memory. Only a few would try to preserve it.[4]

At the dawn of the new century Edward Butler Horne (Kangangi) would arrive on the southern slopes of Mt. Kenya. He was given authority by the British to take control of the Eastern slopes of the mountain where the Meru tribe made their home. He was young but had travelled to Canada and Wyoming late in the 19th Century working as a lumberjack and ranch hand. He was a man of the outdoors. He was born in 1881, one of 8 brothers. He was known as Shorthorn as opposed to his taller brother,

Longhorn. Butler was a fanatical hunter who agreed to travel to Kenya in service to the Crown. He had a capacity for languages and eventually mastered Swahili, Maasai, Embu, Nandi, and eventually, Kimeru.[5]

In 1906, the British took a force of the KAR and started the trek through Embu to Meru country on the southeastern flank of Mt. Kenya. Horne's retinue also was supported by some coastal Swahili and Gikuyu who would help him communicate with the Meru. Horne was part of the original force that had first tried to subdue the Embu some time ago, but now had been made commander for this expedition. Heading north to the heart of Meru country, he eventually set up a permanent headquarters in order to bring this region under British rule.

The Meru had been living in the fertile hills and valleys in the foothills of Mt. Kenya for centuries. Though the Meru clans were known to fight among themselves at times, they had a very evolved culture and a set of rules determined by the Council of Elders. Each age group knew its place, each followed the rules. Infractions of the rules were effectively discouraged by curses imposed by the Witchmen.

The Embu are the tribe between the Gikuyu, to the south, and the Meru, to the north. Their fierce reputation protected them. They had seen whites pass through with the Swahili caravans in the past. The caravans were often accompanied by the Kamba, another coastal people. The whites were labelled *Machunku*, red men. The whites would plunder what they could not bargain for.

Some Embu had returned with tales from the Gikuyu of the shooting sticks which conquered the Gikuyu long before this time. So, when the Embu saw the contingent of KAR led by three British officers approaching, they realized their tribe was in trouble. Conventions of tribal war were not being followed. Women and children were beaten and abused. Even the Gikuyu in the attack were plundering and maiming the Embu. Embu freedom would soon perish. Warriors, though brave, could not fight against the shooting sticks. Entire villages fled into the forest. There was panic. They travelled north to report the catastrophe to the Meru.

To Butler Horne this appeared as a very backward and uncivilized part of the world. His arrival far north of Embu showed his least likable qualities. This would become evident in the meeting with Mbogore M'Mwendo, the foremost commander of Upper Mwimbi. Mbogore was appointed as spokesman for the entire Meru tribe. Horne arrived surrounded by Maasai spearmen. They met at the Nithi River. Caesar had arrived![6]

The Rhythm Of Africa

Log and saw
Panga and earth
Bent back
Pains of birth.

The rhythm of Africa
Is the rhythm of work.

Maize and millet
Rock on stone
Metal and hammer
Muscle and bone!

The rhythm of Africa
Is the rhythm of work.

Basket of coral
Basket of sand
Carried on the head
In Black Man's land.

The rhythm of Africa
Is the rhythm of work.

Dhow and pole
Needle and net
Rope and sail
Dry or wet.

The rhythm of Africa
Is the rhythm of work.

Long and saw
Panga and earth
Bent back
Pains of birth!

CHAPTER 14

NJAGE ENCOUNTERS HORNE (1907)

N jage, the tallest and most muscular of his Age-Set, was a very powerful Ameru *athaka* (warrior). He was respected by his tribe and his father had a great wealth in cattle. Njage enjoyed listening to the elders and learning the folklore of his tribe. The tribe's history, his own history, was filled with adventure and the overcoming of obstacles. Kithingi, his father, had told him how they had migrated for many, many years before reaching this place of plenty: rich mountain soil, thick forest, pleasant weather high above the arid plane. There was bountiful rain and when it didn't fall, the many glacial mountain streams provided irrigation.

Sabari, Njage's great grandfather, just before passing into the realm of the spirits, had told Kithingi about his tribe's migrations. Kithingi had shared some of these accounts with Njage. But so much was missing. Njage wanted to know more. Someday he would see if his grandfather, Muthamia, might tell him more. Only when

he was an Elder would the whole story be revealed to him.
So far Njage knew his ancestors had migrated from
the west to the seacoast and finally settled on the Island
of Mbwaa. He also had learned that eventually they
began leaving the island. That was during the time of the
Nkuthuku and *Ntangi* Age-Sets. These times were shrouded
in the mystery of long ago.

Leaving the island in groups, following the rivers,
passing through arid places, they ultimately came to green
Meru country. Each group chose a different ridge on which
to settle and to establish its own clan. Some even ventured
into the forest to become hunters again.

Their various councils of elders provided the rules of
their life, the divisions of their Age-Sets, and the means of
resolving disputes. Warriors could raid but were required
to show mercy to the enemy once the defeated called out
"Chukua Ngombe!" — "take cows!" They were proud and
powerful which gave them the confidence to be merciful.

Njage also heard accounts of the slave traders and their
caravans which arrived close to this very place in the lower
valley. Arabs, Swahili, and Kamba came to trade for skins,
ivory, and slaves. What stayed in Njage's mind was the
legend of the beautiful Ameru woman, Mahiri. She was the
daughter of their shared ancestor, Lawi. Njage traced his
lineage back to Lawi, as did this Mahiri. The tale told of a
Swahili, named Omari, who saw her and desired her much,
not as a slave, but as a wife. Omari was the trader whose
father owned the caravan. It was decided that Mahiri and
Omari could marry, since Omari was able to provide a great
bride price and that he would treat Mahiri well.

Njage thought that one day he might travel to the great
salt sea and see if he could find descendants of Mahiri. It

was his dream. He would pray to *Murungu* (God) and ask his ancestral *Nkoma* (spirits) for assistance.

Njage was grateful to his ancestors, Sabari, Muthamia, and the other Elders who passed down the tribe's lore as they sat by the fires late at night and recounted their history in sing-song tales. *O, to have the knowledge of an Elder,* he thought. *So Much was only for the ears of the wise Wazee* (*old Men*).

These tales had been repeated time and again, from father to son to grandson, through the ages. This tribal history was thus passed to each generation. Thus, each man of the tribe would know who he was, where he was from, and what was expected of him. Each event was tied to the warrior Age-Set that came into manhood, about fourteen years apart. Thus, the tribe kept an oral time record of events. It kept them connected to their ancestors and taught the young their values. Njage also learned that the Meru were considered a fiercer tribe than the Gikuyu to the south. The Meru had learned and copied much from the Samburu and Maasai, their neighbors to the north and south.

Njage's grandfather, Muthamia, told him of the first white caravan which tried to bargain with the Meru long ago. The caravan was passing from the north toward Gikuyu country but was short on food. The Africans from the caravan tried to engage the Meru elders in discussion, but the Meru refused and sent warriors to patrol the borders of their land. The Somalis in the caravan were ready to fight, but their leader, a white man called Lord Delamere (known to Africans as Lordi D), approached the elders unarmed. He asked to be allowed to pass through Meru country on his way south. Through sign language he persuaded the Meru to trade for food and allow safe passage. The elders were impressed that Lordi D came to them bravely, unarmed. As a result, the Meru capitulated and allowed the caravan to pass, provided they did not interrupt their tribes lives and would go quickly. Muthamia was impressed with this man's bravery and that he spoke the language of the Somalis.[7]

———•••———

Njage's interest in his tribe's history was reignited when he heard of the infamous Kangangi, as Horne was known to the Meru. Horne's war on the Embu to the south was the latest news and gossip among the Meru. Njage had met with some Embu warriors who suspected that the KAR would be coming north. Njage's mind was racing. He spent time contemplating how he and the tribe should react to the coming invasion. He did not have to wait very long.

Butler Horne's greatest challenge occurred at the Nithi River. He, in full military regalia, riding the largest white horse the tribesmen had ever seen, proceeded toward the river. Horne, surrounded by the contingent of the KAR, Maasai spearmen, along with Gichuru, his Gikuyu translator, were an imposing sight. To Njage and the Meru it was as if an evil *Nkoma* (spirit) had descended on them from above. Njage did not fear, but his mind was overwhelmed to its core. He sensed that his life would never be the same again.

Horne knew some Kiswahili. But he began in English, asking Gichuru to translate into Kimeru:

"*Muga*, I am Gichuru here to speak the words of this *Mingereza* (Englishman), Sir Edward Butler Horne"

"*Mugamano*, I am Njage, a Meru warrior. I have been appointed spokesman by and for the elders," replied Njage.

Gichuru translated, "Bwana wants to speak with the elders. Where are the warriors?"

"They are in the forest. The elders are on their way."

"Ask them all to assemble quickly!"

"We have sent for them. See, there in the trees. They approach."

Soon many warriors could also be heard approaching. They were chanting and striking their shields with their spears. A horde soon appeared and stood jumping in place by the trees. The elders followed and sat in a circle in front of the warriors, away from the trees.

Mbogore M'Mwendo, war leader of upper Mwimbi, also arrived with the elders. Gichuru continued to translate as Horne spoke in English.

"Warriors, I have come to speak with your elders. I come in peace to bring word from the Great British King and Emperor! I come to rule, not to visit."

At this there was a great commotion. The elders looked perplexed and the warriors became inflamed with anger. Horne now saw his opportunity for maximum drama. Sitting on his great white stead, he pointed his rifle at a large bull behind Njage. With one shot he downed the beast and proclaimed: *"Nyama!"* Meaning "Meat for all of you!"

The warriors now infuriated began their war chant, jumping and raising their spears.

Now Horn shouted to them with authority, "Gichuru, say to them this is meat for the feast which we will celebrate. Tell them I will be appointing Chiefs and giving them rules. First ask some warriors if their spears can pierce one of their shields."

Njage spoke almost immediately: "This is impossible! Our shields are very strong."

Horne now gave another order: "Tell 5 men to stand their shields upright in a row, one behind the other. There. By the trees!"

Once they were arranged, Horne riddled them with bullet holes and the shields fell to the ground, shattered. There was silence. It was as if all the warriors and elders realized the significance: their world was no longer the same.

Horne now spoke again, "Warriors, stand aside! I come here to speak with your elders. I come in peace. You will turn in your spears and weapons. There will be no more raids, so says the Great British King!"[8]

More commotion. The elders faces proclaimed their profound irritation with this threat to their authority. At this a great cry arose among the warriors: "How shall we survive? Feed ourselves? Protect our families from the Maasai?"

"Through trade and work. You will begin by building my great road. Men will dig the way and women will fill baskets with dirt and rocks. This is how you will live! The King will protect your families," replied the mounted Englishman, the imperial Kangangi.

At this the warriors chanted louder: "Warriors do not dig! Warriors do not dig!"

Njage tried to explain, "Kangangi, digging and planting is women's work! Men do not dig. The custom is for Murran to protect and be served. Warriors never dig!"

Horne pulled the horses reins so that it raised its front legs high and then shot into the air and proclaimed: "You will do the King's bidding, or we will send more KAR. The road building begins in two days!"

And so, this was the beginning of the end to Meru freedom and the destruction of a thriving way of life. Their culture would be dismantled, piece by piece, in the name of progress. Slowly families would be ripped apart. Children would forget their heritage, and they would be no better off than slaves.

Horne continued, "I will appoint a chief for each region. I will choose one of you to be Chief. I prefer someone who can speak Kiswahili so we can communicate. Whom do you choose? O, I like this man there," pointing at Njage.

Mbogore, the war leader, agreed. He knew Njage would tell him the truth and also be able to understand the real meaning behind Kangangi's English words.

Now Horne approached Njage, "Njage come. Take this kanga (blanket). This black kanga is the symbol of your authority and power. You will give my order again: 'There must be no more raids!'"

Horne continued, "So, Njage, you will be my Boy here in Muthambi (southern Meru country). Later, I will take you to Mutindwa, where I will build my fort."

"It depends on the conditions you place on me!" Njage emphasized in forceful Kiswahili.

"These are the conditions. You will translate for me, teach me Kimeru, and give the elders and the people my orders."

"I would, if the orders are not extreme. But what is there for me to gain?"

"You will be called Chief of Chiefs and you will receive gifts if you do my bidding."

Njage thought long and hard, but finally agreed. He did not understand this word Chief. The Meru only had Councils of Elders and Witchmen who ruled the tribe.

However, he agreed because he knew the tribe could not fight with spears, but he knew the elders had their ways of dealing with men, even powerful men, and there were the Witchmen, their curses, and their potions. In this way he would learn how best to deal with these white men who said they were conquering his people. He loved his people but needed to find ways to combat this new terror. The Meru were strong and intelligent people and they knew that time was on their side. He knew the English, like Kangangi, would tire, and the Meru would be victorious in the end.

"Yes, I agree. I will do your bidding."

So Njage was appointed as Chief. He was given the black blanket of authority and was told his main duty was a go-between for the elders and the British Officers who would be transmitting the orders of the King. He was asked to find others from each clan who were strong and brave warriors who would be Chiefs of their own clans. It would be preferable if they knew some Kiswahili. Njage was to be the leader of the Chiefs in Meru, Chief of Chiefs.

Horne now took Gichuru aside and told him what he was to relay to the elders. Horne, himself, spent time with Njage since he understood Kiswahili. He instructed him in the duties of a Chief. Gichuru found the elders quiet but skeptical. They asked Gichuru how it was in Kikuyu land and he told them that the rules were strict, that the Gikuyu went deep into the forest when they needed to conduct their rites, but that it was easier to not enrage the British. He told them the many changes that must follow. The cessation of cattle raiding and fighting by warriors, the institution of work in place of warrior hood, and many, many, more changes. The warriors would be required to dig a road up the ridges to the next village, and the women would be required to fill baskets with mud and sand using their hands to smooth the roadbed. At this the Elders protested again, but Gichuru calmed them and told them that the wrath of the British is great. He had seen whipping, jailing, and worse. He urged the Meru elders to find ways to live their life as before the Englishman, Kangangi, had arrived.

In a few days, Horne and the caravan would continue on to the next village and repeat the process to establish a presence. Finally, they arrived in North Imenti at a place called Mutindwa. It was a place used by warriors to practice defense against the Maasai and Turkana. It was by the sacred fig tree. Horne had men fell large trees and construct a Canadian type log cabin. This would be his headquarters.

Gichuru remained with Horne for six months. During this time, he learned much of the Meru. He made many friends. He found that they were not so different from his own people, that they had a similar diet, that they enjoyed the same simple things in life.

Horne was very pleased with his selection of Mutindwa for his headquarters. It has located on a high, level place with a fine view in all directions. Looking down away from Mt. Kenya you could see the vast northern plains to Samburu land. Looking upward, there were enormous forests providing building materials. The land was rich volcanic earth which provided the tribes with abundant harvests. *Yes*, thought Horne, *this is a very fine place!* After this period Gichuru was given leave to go home to his family. As he did so, Horne told him that he hoped he would return some day to assist him in teaching the

Meru people. He headed toward home, better informed of the white man's ways and plans, but more confused than ever. The appearance of the white men was increasing the African people's confusion and suffering. It was presenting him and them with a great dilemma.

As he began the long trek back, Gichuru's mind was overwhelmed by all he had seen and heard. He now had time to think about what was happening. He was conflicted by the part he was playing and confused about what would result. It was all happening so quickly. He was helping to destroy a culture as his was being destroyed. These tribes had survived for thousands of years through much hardship and suffering. In the past people of individual tribes knew their place and standing in the tribe, who they were, and where they had come from. This new world might have advantages. Advantages like he had had — learning new languages, seeing the great Iron Rhino, the building of Nairobi in the swamp. But what were they giving up? Their freedom. Their culture. What would be his ultimate role and fate? How would he be judged by his tribe, family, and white men? Questions, Questions, Questions!

CHAPTER 15

LAIKISAT COMES TO NAIROBI (1905)

L aikisat and his friend, Letegall, agreed that when they would be near the great *Ol Doinyo Keri* (Mt. Kenya), they would approach it from the south, where it was said that the white men were busy building a great village, where the Iron Rhino stopped. He had seen this great Rhino travel like a snake only from a distance. It roared like a beast and followed the same path each time. The Witchmen had warned them to stay away because it was a cursed thing. Those who approached too closely would be pursued by evil spirits.

But they were enticed by what they had heard and what tales Lorran, Laikisat's cousin, had told them. They wanted to see it for themselves. So off they went on foot walking in rhythm like pharaohs across the plain and following the river into the highlands.

In the distance they saw it! The great *Ol Donyo Keri* (Mt. Kenya) grew closer and larger until they spotted the village. It was so different from theirs, not of natural materials like mud and grasses. The huts were all connected with wooden covered areas above a wooden walkway. All were arranged in a long, straight stretch with many corners and no round parts. The town stretched so far that it encompassed the horizon. There were many structures higher than they had ever seen in their lives. Most were taller than a man, and some higher than a giraffe. Between the rows of buildings were paths that were covered in a red substance that was hard like rock. No dust or mud underfoot.

On the outskirts they entered a compound fenced with a gate. An African guard at the gate asked a question, but they could not understand what he said. They realized that it was the language of the mountain people, the Gikuyu. Laikisat knew his own language Maa, and a few words of Kiswahili that he had picked up from other Maasai who had talked with Arab traders.

Slowly with hand signals they managed to communicate. The two explained where they were from and that they wanted to see this new place. The guard told them its name was Nairobi, which was a name they knew in their own language and meant a place of cool water. The guard would take them to see an important man who could talk to them in their own language and show them some interesting places.

The guard disappeared for a bit while Laikisat and Letegall sat on the ground and consumed a bit of dried meat, which they carried in their leather sacks. Soon the guard returned with a young man called Gichuru. He introduced himself in their language and told them they were welcome to spend this day and the next with him. Gichuru took them to his home, a modest wood building with a thatched roof and told them they could camp at his shamba (farm field) under the large shade trees. Later he would show them some places and how this village worked.

The two days were filled with many new sights. The two men where awestruck and could not comprehend all the complexity of life there. Gichuru was a friendly man whom they came to admire because he could not only speak to them, but also intelligently to the many different people they encountered. Gichuru was equally comfortable with the whites, as with the members of other African tribes. He seemed important and the two Maasai wanted to stay with him to learn more, but they knew they needed to return to their duties in Maasai land. Gichuru invited them to visit again and bring some things for trading purposes. He suggested objects that would appeal to the white people. Laikisat also invited Gichuru to visit them on the plains.

As the men parted the next day, Laikisat and Letegall were pleased and impressed but also bewildered by what they had seen. Most of all they were happy to have met this man and now counted him as their friend.

Gichuru returned to his office where he was a government clerk. He was impressed with his new friends. Gichuru knew the Maasai were quite independent and this was an opportunity to build a bridge. He realized that there would be benefits to both sides for trade. Building this friendship would also fit into his ultimate plans.

He had found a woman, Wanjiku, from his own tribe whom he planned to take as his first wife. She was beautiful, intelligent, and hard working. His father, Kahara, had already approached her father to speak about the dowry. They lived in Molo on the other side of the Rift Valley near Kahara's brother, who was a trader. While he still was a boy, he and his father had had a great adventure. They travelled

on the Iron Rhino down the Rift and up the other side of
the Valley. That was when he first met Wanjiku. She had
made quite an impression on the young Gichuru.

Right now, this was uppermost in Gichuru's mind, but
he knew he must also fulfill his job commitments in the
government office. He realized he was balancing his life
like he used to do when he tried to walk on large tree
limbs as a child. Sometimes he succeeded but at others he
fell with a hard thump to the ground. The trick was not
to lose balance.

CHAPTER 16

LAIKISAT RETURNS (1905)

A year later, Laikisat and Letegall decided that they would return to meet Gichuru and bring him some trading goods. They wanted some of the goods they saw in the great village: for instance, they wanted some green plants that they used for potions and some implements of iron. They were bringing objects that they knew the *Wazungu* (Europeans) wanted — some stones like glass, some pelts of antelope, and some animal teeth. They hoped that these would be valued.

They set out and walked for four days to reach the meeting place that Gichuru had arranged. He was not there when they first arrived, but they inquired and were told to wait. Gichuru returned the next day.

"*Suba*, Laikisat and Letegall. How are you both?" Gichuru greeted them.

"We are fit! We have brought you some things."

"These fine stones will be prized especially by the *Wazungu* (Europeans)!" replied Gichuru, awestruck.

"Good we could make a trade for some goods that you have, and we need."

Gichuru was thankful. "Come now to my *shamba* (farm) where you can rest and feast. You will see many changes that I have made."

They walked for about an hour or so to Gichuru's *shamba*. As they approached the green shamba with the lush forest trees, Gichuru said, "Here are my cows and my maize plants. I also have started some coffee trees. It will take some time before they bear."

"Your place is very green. Much greener than our much drier place."

Gichuru smiled, "Yes it stays fairly green all year, even in the dry season. There, you can rest under those large trees. It will be cool. Yes, this is fine land, but the *Wazungu* are taking the even better land higher up. They are growing much coffee and tea in large plantations at the better altitudes. We are barred from those areas."

Laikisat pondered a bit. "I do not know the *Wazungu*. My people are happy with our land and we do not want our ways to change. A *Wazungu* man with a long white beard came to our place and tried to persuade the elders to pray to a new god. We drove him off because we did not want to lose our ways and because we thought it might anger *Ngai* (God) and cause a drought."

Gichuru replied, "There are many White God People here. I even was educated by them. I gained many useful skills, like writing. Many are kind. I even accepted their god, but I have also kept my Gikuyu ways. We go deep into the forest when we practice our rites. I need to learn and know all I can about the whites so my people can contend with the invaders. I am learning how they think. You too must learn how they think. I have heard that they have made a pact with the *Wajerumani* (Germans) to the south to restrict you, the Maasai, to certain areas, and prevent you from some highlands. You will soon find out. Prepare yourselves. Beware!"

"Our people will not be happy with this, but your advice is very good. You are already helping us in what you have told me. We too wish to know more."

Gichuru now made his proposition, "Let us make a pact to meet, say every two full moons."

"Yes, this is good. We can trade and exchange our knowledge."

"I have business in Meru country, so if you do not find me, you can trade with my father, Kahara. He is old but has all his wits. I will leave a message with him if I am not here."

"Agreed."

Laikisat and Letegall were happy with their new friend. They now knew how to improve the standing of their people. They would help each other learn about these *wazungu* (strangers) that were coming to their land. They might find ways to see that the wazungu would not gain all the advantages of their ancestral land. The pact to meet was a good idea. They would learn and wait. Wait for the appropriate time. Wait in the hope that their children would prosper one day like the *Wazungu*.

CHAPTER 17

HOLY MEN AND DISCORD BREWING (1906-1909)

Years passed. Gichuru's trade with the Maasai and the whites prospered. Laikisat returned many times and they both were learning how to deal with changes. Gichuru had even gone back to Meru for 6 months to help Horne with convincing the Meru Chiefs to listen to him.

In 1909 while Gichuru was still at Fort Meru he met two new Wazungu holy men who had just arrived. John B. Griffiths, a Welshman, had travelled to Embu in 1906 and was in Fort Meru in 1907 with Butler Horne. It wasn't until 1909 that Griffiths was given permission by the British to establish a mission. There had been much consternation among different mission societies over this. The Anglicans, Methodists, and Catholics were all wishing to get a foothold in what they considered fertile land to plant their faiths. The British finally drew borders where each faith could establish its own mission. Many times, these borders divided clans and families. In 1909 Griffiths and

Mimmack, his assistant, along with twenty-four Gikuyu porters, traveled the 171 miles from Nairobi, through Nyeri to Fort Meru on footpaths and tracks.[9]

In Mutindwa (Fort Meru) Griffiths spoke with Gichuru and was impressed with him. It was common to use Gikuyu converts as teachers, since they were some of the first converts among Africans. Griffiths was also very glad that Gichuru had been educated at the Scottish Mission in Kabete. He asked Gichuru if he would consider returning and bringing some of his old school mates to help at the school they were going to establish. Gichuru told them that he would return next year after the rains.

Gichuru also met with Njage before he left. They discussed what was occurring in Nairobi and the talk of trouble brewing between white tribes in Europe and also in the African colonies. One night by the fire, they were startled by movement in the thick brush. First they prepared to fight a wild animal, but as they stared into the darkness they could see the outline of two tall men!

"Who goes there?" Njage yelled fiercely.

"Show yourselves or prepare to face our *rungus* (wooden maces)!" Shouted Gichuru.

The two red figures walked slowly forward until Njage and Gichuru could better see the faces of the two emerge from the bush. Their red ochre shone as Njage held the torch closer to the two men. The strangers' ochre glimmered in the firelight.

"It is us, Laikisat and Letegall. We have come to talk."

"O, Laikisat, you have surprised us. We thought you two were leopards coming to have us for their dinner! *Karibu!* It has been over 4 rains since we last met and shared the kill. I have missed your trade," replied the astonished Njage.

Gichuru, amazed: "Laikisat, you, here!"

Laikisat: "Gichuru? And you with Njage? How Ngai shines on our friendship! We all find each other. He might have some plan for us."

They all stared quietly at each other at this astonishing coincidence. Finally, Njage spoke, "I did not realize that we all knew each other! We are fortunate! Fortunate to be *marafiki* (friends). Come sit by our warm fire. The night cold sweeps in from the mountains."

Laikisat responded first, "I have had a busy life preparing for my bride price. My warrior days will last four or six more rains. We have been occupied with a few cattle raids recently. I come now because we Maasai overhear much about the *Wazungu's* (Europeans) troubles in the south, near *Ngagi Ngai* (Kilimanjaro). The Wajerumani (Germans) have many warriors near that mountain. Some of them are African Askari."

Gichuru nodded, agreeing, "Yes our Governor also speaks about this, but he thinks the troubles will remain near their homelands, *Ujerumani* (Germany) and *Uingereza* (England). He says the troubles will not come to us. He is being pressured to prepare but is reluctant for his people to have to fight."

Njage invited them again, "Laikisat and Letegall, come sit by the fire. Warm yourselves. I will ask my wife to have women bring food. We can talk into the night."

In the years since Horne had arrived and Njage had been appointed chief of chiefs for the Meru, he had married. Kithingi, Njage's father had collected the bride price, and Njage was pleased that he had chosen Njuri. Njage had known her since he was a young boy, and now was happy to be wed to her. They soon would have a family.

The next morning, they rose to a very gray heavy sky. A sure sign that the short rains would begin that afternoon. They left with heavy hearts, pledging to keep their ears and eyes open and report back to each other as soon as they heard or saw something. They tentatively arranged to meet after the end of the long rains.

During Gichuru's long trek back to the capital he pondered what they had spoken about and how his life had become one of travel and education. He learned more and more about the colonials and their god. Every chance he got he tried to draw analogies between the Africans and the missionary's ideas and to look for similarities in belief. He was smart enough to know that there were many ways for people to be good. He knew that Africans had large hearts and showed much mercy, and that the whites had not invented these qualities. He tried to show Njage how to be a good Chief and not anger the elders. It was a very difficult road, but they both were trying as best they could.

Gichuru also worried about Laikisat and his Maasai. They were the most independent of the three tribes and had much to lose. Their grazing rights had already been limited. Gichuru knew that the Governor and Legislative Council were planning new restrictions. He knew this might lead to Maasai anger. He would try to listen and warn Laikisat.

Back in Nairobi Gichuru heard more talk about the Germans. They controlled the south part of the Maasai land. Historically, this area was referred to as German East Africa or Tanganyika. Recently the Africans there had rebelled when forced to work on the cotton plantations. The Germans were ruthless in quelling what became known as the *Maji Maji* Rebellion. More than one-quarter million Africans died in the uprising and the following famine.

Gichuru realized that the English were not as severe as the Germans, but, also, that his tribe was more accommodating to the English. He worried how long the status quo would hold and he wondered what the future would bring.[10]

CHAPTER 18

NJAGE (1908)

N jage had been working closely with Bwana Horne and Reverend Worthington, the new White God Person, who was building a church and school. The elders and warriors were grumbling at him constantly over the many changes occurring daily. The only happy people, it seemed, were the chosen warriors who lived with Horne at Fort Meru. They were the ones who carried out his wishes if there were disturbances or dealt with tribesmen who did not follow instructions. They were disliked by the Meru. Though all spears and weapons were now forbidden, the Fort Warriors of Horne could carry *rungus* (wooden maces) and they were not afraid of using them.

Njage saw that many of these rules were starting to cause ill affects among his people. Recall that in Meru tradition warriors were forbidden to partake in drink or sex during this stage of life. Their sole job was protection of the tribe and going on raids for cattle. Warriors had set rules during cattle raids. If a man was defeated and near to being harmed or killed, he could cry out *"Ngua Ng'ombe! (Take cattle!)"* and he would be spared. It was a code of the warrior morality. These rules were enforced by the elders. They now had been stripped of power. Recall that Horne had forbidden raids and had confiscated spears and shields, placing them all in Fort Meru.

The warriors' excess energy now started to bother them, and they found solace in drink and finding young women who would spend time with them. At first there was just close contact, but nothing out of the ordinary. However, as time went on, more and more sexual relations were occurring and more and more out-of-wedlock pregnancies. The older women became concerned as did the Rev. Worthington. The children of these relations were unwanted and the women ostracized by the tribe. Worthington saw a possible solution to this problem and an advantage to his mission. He began offering to take the children in and training them as Christians in the new school he had established. The other Meru potential congregants came and went, and the missionaries saw orphans as a godsend to have students who could not leave. Njage's mind reeled.

He thought *How could these God people think that this was sent by Murungu (God) as a prize to them? These evils destroying the Meru must be sent by the evil Nkoma (spirits). Murungu should be protecting his people. These evils came upon his Meru people because the wazungu (foreigners) were having the people ignore the old ways. The warriors' spirits had been destroyed! Now all the taboos governing their lives were gone! The Nkoma (spirits) were punishing the tribe!*

As the problem increased, some of the older women tried to protect their young girls by fixing potions and beating them until they miscarried. It was better to have a young girl who could then marry than to have one no man would want as a wife. The missionaries and Horne had stiff punishments for pregnancy, and, especially, abortions.

Imprisonment was unknown before. Now these penalties fell hard on the Meru, especially the older women and girls. Not used to being left in a room locked up all day caused them to lose hope, and many fell ill. Some even died. It was a cruel and unusual punishment for these people.

Horne then tried to remove the power of the ruling Councils of Elders. He replaced the elders with his selected Meru men. The Elders, however, continued to meet in secret and direct the tribe. This added to the friction between the Meru rulers and the colonials. All these problems were very rare before the coming of the white man. Now it was tearing the intricate fabric of social cohesion into shreds!

The Leader, of the Council of Elders, Mukanga, summoned Njage: "*Muga*, Njage! Sit with us. We and the *Nkoma* (Spirits) are being disturbed by the changes being brought upon us. We are confused and dismayed. Even though you are still young and not near an elder's age, we are taking you into our confidence. This is highly unusual, but so are these times. You must know certain events since you have so much interaction with Kangangi (Horne) and the others. Only in this way will you be able to understand who you are and where you come from. You must know our legends – you, especially, the proud descendent of Lawi!"

"*Mugamano, Wazee! Asante* (Thank you) for your trust. You honor me. I always wish to learn. The combined wisdom of our elders is great, and you are always just. I have learned some about the brave Lawi who first arrived on *Kirimara* (Mt. Kenya), but I wish to know more, more of the other great men."

"Your job is difficult and trying. We know. We know

how upset you are with the destruction of our old ways,"
replied Mukanga, "Long ago our Meru clans departed from
other Bantu during the great migrations. We have kept
our traditions through our travels and in spite of violence.
Our songs tell us much of those days."

The drummer began a quiet beat as Mukanga began
his chant:

"So dim is the long ago!
With word and song, we travel
Travel back,
Travel far,
Relying on the endless chain
Of what each elder to each younger told.

Places now dry, were wet,
And forests, larger and thicker
And Murungu (God) let life, all life
Multiply and prosper.

But violence and cruelty
Became a great pressure
That forced men to trek
From deep forests
And great lake waters,
Along wide rivers,
Over hills and planes.

They hid from strange nomads,
Who travelled on camels,
On camels who carried
Houses on their humps.

The men tall, slender and brown,
Traveled with herds and their women
Who did not walk,
But flowed in shear dresses,
Veils, scarves
Flapping in the wind!

Our people, our Meru,
Were weary and hungry
And nearly exhausted.
When suddenly.
Surprisingly
They came upon it
Upon it suddenly!
From horizon to horizon,
They saw it stretching
Saw the water,
The great salt sea!

And 'midst the sea,
They found an island,
Vacant land
By sea surrounded,
And called it Mbwaa (Manda)
And there,
There amidst the palms and mangrove
Would make their home.

On this isle amidst the sea,
They found abundance,
Abundance for all,
From land and sea!
A place of safety from invasion,
Happy place for many, many generations."

Here he paused and drank deeply from his gourd. Mukanga's eyes were glassy as the dimming beams of sunlight reflected off them. All the others were mesmerized by the deep memory of their beginnings.

Njage looked at Mukanga and the others and felt surprised but privileged to be hearing of the past. "A great salt sea! I cannot imagine it. How I wish to behold it someday. Our people ventured so far with so much suffering. But now we stay in one place, close to our mountain and rarely venture far. What brave and adventurous ancestors!"

Mukanga agreed, "E-e-e, but you will see how much braver the descendants of the travelers were. They would face many trials!"

Mukanga stared at the night sky, the multitude of stars, and the great streak of light which was like the milk flowing from his cows, or the long line of ancestors stretching backward through time and into the future. The sky and the stars helped him remember. After a long pause, he continued:

"Peaceful people came to trade
Large boats from north and east
Came over sea and over waves
Through the salted sea they came.
Ceramic, metal objects,
Silver and gold coin
They brought across the water,
Exchanged for our ivory, ebony,
And exotic beasts.

Their skin, brown,
Almost white.

They came in sandals,
Wearing white.
We thought them gods,
Or come from gods!

The god-like leaders
Were obeyed.
The others, attentive
And obedient
To their every need
And word.

Others inscribed thin animal skins
With diagrams and marks
Using large bird quills.
They did not linger
But southward went,
Writing and observing,
Never to be seen again.

Later, much later
Some short men came,
Short with slanted eyes,
To observe and to trade
But quickly left.

Then with wind and storm
From the northeast, others came.
First, peacefully to trade,
But later took Bantu wives and slaves
To work and serve.

They called themselves Warabu (Arabs)
Their speech we called, Kiarabu.
They said they came in peace to us the Bantu.
They settled mostly on the farther coast,
Also wrote on skins
But with much finer and more intricate marks
Which even some of our Bantu learned.

But then began their travels inland far
To trade and gather more and more.
They gathered men,
They gathered women,
They gathered babes
From distant tribes to enslave!"

Now the drummer began a louder and more rapid beating of the large drum and Mukanga's voice filled with anger also grew louder:

"With violence they gathered them
With violence, beat them
They herded them like cattle
And like cattle sent them far!
Away on boats so far!
Lost to us, to their kin,
Lost forever, never seen again!

Trade, plantations grew larger,
Our fear, greater, deeper.
Would they enslave us? Send us far?
Send us south, send us north?
Take our women, beat them,

Make them slaves?
How to protect our tribe!
How to survive?"

The drummer's sound returned to a more moderate sound:

"The Councils met and sat,
Thought for many days,
For many days discussed,

Sat, until with voice unanimous
Decided:
Leave they would
Though their children here grew strong
And life was good
Leave they would
To insure the tribe's survival.

So, they set the plan:
Different clans at different times
Would leave the isle
Some at dawn, some at dusk, some at night
In the darkest night.

But how?
How to cross such high waters?
Witchmen were consulted.
Witchmen danced, sacrificed the goats,
Read the omens, the signs
And waited.
Finally, spoke the Nkoma (Spirits)!

'We will move the waters.
Wait,
Wait 'till the moon is full.
Only then will you leave!
With your goats, with your cattle,
Only then will you leave!
With your wives, your elders
Only then will you leave!'

They waited.
For the fullness of the moon,
They waited.
'Till the rushing of the sea
Like a river waters rushing
A rising and a parting!

All men were stupefied,
Marveled, astonished!
Where once was sea
A dry track appeared.

The first clan gathered,
Gathered their children,
Their wives, their elders.
And stepped on the track,
And crossed,
Crossed from the isle
To the other side.

As suddenly as parted
The sea flooded the track
While from the mainland

The astonished clan
Safely stared back!

This was repeated after some time
As the tide came in and subsided.
The clans were thus divided,
Divided by time,
Divided by color,
Red faced at dawn, at mid-day white,
And black at night!

Each clan was saved
And the tribe survived
Because of the good of the Witchman
And of the Nkoma!
Now began the arduous trek
The trek of the Ngaa
For that was the name of the Bantu
Before they arrived at our home,
The present-day Meru.

They trekked along the great rivers
Toward uplands, climbing higher.
They fled the violence of the isle
By the great saltwater,
Until the time of Mukuruma
When they first beheld our Kirimara (Mt. Kenya)!"

Mukanga's voice now was fading. He was exhausted and excused himself for his eyes were heavy and sleep was calling him.

Another Elder finished the story, "And so they trekked

for many years until they reached the foothills here where they could behold *Kirimara* and *Murungu's* (God's) white cloud. They knew this was the place that He wanted them to settle and prosper. Truly this was a sign that the ancestors were smiling on their decision! *Murungu* had led them, and their decision had been blessed by the *Nkoma!"*

Njage's eyes were filled with pride that the Elders had entrusted him with this knowledge. He was still just a warrior and these legends were only for those who would carry the secrets of the tribe. *"Asante, Wazee! Asante,* Mukanga! You have filled me with pride and understanding. I am grateful you have entrusted me with this knowledge. I will carry it in my heart."

"Njage, we wish to inspire you because we know your work with the *Wazungu* (Europeans) is very hard. It is different from fighting another warrior or a beast. You cannot use your spear or your muscles, but you must corral every inner strength of your mind and your wits. Help all your people and know that we stand with you. Remember the *Nkoma* of your ancestors are with you also. Go now in peace," Mukanga stood over Njage and blest him with his spittle.

Njage was inspired by the confidence of the elders'but saddened by destruction of the Meru's traditions. He himself continued to follow the elders' directives but felt like he was walking on a fine line. The elders' and Horne were pushing and pulling him in opposing directions. One false step and he would perish! He was waiting for the end of his warriorhood, so that he could take a wife and enjoy starting a family. He still followed the tribe's custom of not having relations with a woman until he passed out of the warrior Age-Set. A couple, before marriage, could at best only have limited intimacy. This was the custom that prevented pregnancy and ostracism. Lately many of his Age-Set were ignoring the customs entirely. It was destroying the couple's mutual respect needed to maintain the social fabric of the family and tribe.

Njage hoped he soon would be able to marry Njuri. She lived not far away in the town of Igogi. He was looking forward to this stage of his life. And as old age approached, he hoped to enjoy the prestige of being an elder.

And for this reason, he thought. *I hope that what is happening today will pass. There are many Nkoma (Spirits) around us now. More and more the people are relying on libations offered to the good ancestors and also on the spirit protectors to keep the evil away to restore balance. This is the traditional way of my people!*

This is where Njage placed his hope.

The next few years passed much as before. He worked with Horne and the Reverend and he extended his knowledge of the foreigners, of the mission teachings, and of both Kiswahili and English. The elders were glad that he was their spokesman, even though they grumbled at Njage. He worried about his role as a go-between.

Within the year Njage was scheduled to complete the warrior stage. Finally, he and his Age-Set would graduate to junior elders and married life. Though many had broken with tradition, Njage was one of the few who continued to respect his culture. His father had completed the negotiations for the bride price. At the end of the year he happily married Njuri and they settled on a *shamba* (farm) not far from Horne's fort and the mission station in Mutindwa (Fort Meru).

CHAPTER 19

GICHURU AND THE GOVERNOR (1905-1908)

Sir James Sadler had arrived in East Africa as Consul-General of the British Protectorate of Somaliland in 1898. In 1902 he became Commissioner in Uganda. In late 1905 he was appointed the first Governor of the British East African Protectorate when he moved to Nairobi.[11]

That's when Gichuru first met him. Gichuru felt very important at the ceremony as he translated his speeches into Kiswahili, and then was asked by the Gikuyu elders to explain what was occurring. This was December 12, 1905, when Nairobi became the capital of the British East African Protectorate and Sadler was installed as Governor.

Through the entire year of 1907, the Gikuyu had watched the construction of an imposingly large Government House. It was located on the road called Sixty Street, which ran perpendicular to Queen Victoria Way. Gichuru could just make out the top of the building from his house up on the hills. The British were digging in their heals even more.

One day in 1908 Sadler summoned Gichuru to his office.

"Good morning Sir."

"Good morning, Boy. I need to call a *Baraza Kuu* (Main Meeting) of all the elders and chiefs from Gikuyu land. Have them assemble in the park in a week's time. The Ruling Council and the King require a new system of accounting for travel of Africans. All men will be required to carry a *Kitambulisho* (Identity Card). We need to be able to track movement of peoples."

Gichuru was stunned. "Sir, this *Kitambulisho* will not be accepted easily! My people have always travelled freely to different villages and tribes to trade and visit friends and relatives. There will be much protest on this removal of freedom."

Sadler, with consternation written on his face, said, "I understand. But this is the directive! This will be the law. The men must wear a *Kitambulisho* around their necks at all times! It is out of my hands. Call the *Baraza* and I will deal with it!"

"I will tell them. Good day."

"Good day. Tell me when it has been arranged."

"Yes, Sir."

Gichuru left with great foreboding and immediately started sending runners with the directive. He was convinced that there would be protests. He knew it would take many months before they could execute their mission, and he would tell the elders this. His people were being treated like animals, like dogs having to wear neck collars and dog tags!

BOOK 3:

WAR

CHAPTER 20

WAR PREPARATION AND MORE TAX (1914)

T he years passed and Gichuru travelled to Meru to see Njage and teach at the mission school and Laikisat came to trade. Gichuru did not complain. He was happy to have made these good friends who were soul mates. He had overheard the Governor talking about the generals wanting to increase the number of men in the KAR because of the German and Askari (African regulars) troops near Kilimanjaro. The generals were also inviting the Indian Expeditionary Force. Lord Delamere was constantly in and out of the office having conferences. Gichuru knew that Lord Delamare had a force of Maasai warriors who admired him. Something was brewing.

Gichuru was called in to Sir Henry Belfield's office. He was apprehensive. When Sadler had called him years before to tell the elders about the *Kitambulisho* (Identity Card), there had been much dissatisfaction and some Gikuyu had even moved into the forest and not registered. It must be that another directive was on its way.

Governor Belfield noticed Gichuru approaching through his office window. "Good day. I have a duty for you."

"Yes, Sir."

"I want you to call a *Baraza Kuu* (Main Meeting) of all the chief elders of the Gikuyu. We need a great Counsel representing all areas in a month's time. They need to come from all the areas - from Kijabe, Thika, Nyeri, Nanyuki, as far as Nyahururu and beyond. We have major business to discuss with the elders."

"I will send runners today for a meeting here in one month's time. We can meet below the great fig tree near Dagoretti."

The day came and the elders from all the tribes and some warriors gathered beneath the great fig tree sacred to the tribe. The tree where the *Nkoma* (Spirits) of the ancestors could be summoned.

When the elders were assembled, they chose Gothoro as their main representative.

The Governor began and Gichuru translated, "My good Gikuyu brothers, greetings! We have come as emissaries of the great King George in Britain. As you have heard there is a great war in Europe, and it is here also. We must not allow the *Wajerumani* (Germans) to take over your lands. There are many expenses to pay for this war and for supplies. These *Wajerumani* (Germans) are close by Kilimanjaro. They are even now attacking some of the villages and settlements on our side of Kilimanjaro. We need your help to defeat them. The great King is asking each of us to pay more for protection and assistance - two rupees each or some livestock for each hut. This increase in the *Kodi* (Hut Tax) will help us a great deal. We are also asking for each male of fighting age to register to assist us in fighting in the war."

As soon as he finished, there were cries of protest, the warriors started jumping and yelling that the British had no right to tax the land of their ancestors and that they would not stand for an increase. The elders sat but grumbled and clicked their tongues in disapproval. It took a long time for the rumblings to quiet down. Finally, one of the most respected elders rose and tried to quiet the crowd.

Gichuru translated this for Gothoro:

"For those of you from afar, I am known as the Elder Gothoro. I have lived many seasons, too many to count. Some of you warriors are my great grandchildren. I have seen many things. Arab caravans taking away riches and slaves. I have wandered with my clan until we came to this rich land where we now live. I have seen the coming of the Iron Rhino, of the white fathers and schooling, and of many things. Times will change no matter what we do. I know that you *Waingereza* (English) are not perfect men, but I also know that the *Wajerumani* (Germans) are worse. They killed many Africans years ago in the *Maji Maji* Rebellion. We know you. We have no perfect choice, we must choose.

"Governor, I have lived here for many generations, and first you tell us you need to protect us. Now you need our help. You change your words to suit your wishes. You have already taken some of our men for the *Kariakor* (Carrier Corps). What will you give us for our support?"

Now the Governor started to speak and Gichuru translated.

"I respect your people. You are brave and have allowed us to take some of the vacant land for our farms and towns. We wish to work with you as brothers. You have no power against the shooting *rungus* (rifles) or the flying birds (war planes), which drop fire and destruction. We must fight the *Wajerumani* (Germans) together and I promise you will be allowed to remain safe in your *shambas* (fields)."

Gothoro thought for a while, then addressed Belfield, "Bwana, you give us what is already ours. If we accept this added *Kodi* (Tax), you will protect our women and children if the war comes closer, and when it is done, can we return to living without this *Kodi*?"

"We will protect you, but I cannot say what the Great King will decide, but I promise you we will hold another *Baraza* at the end of the war."

Gothoro was silent for a great while. Then he began again, "We will hold council tonight and I will return with our answer when we are done."

"This is fair. It is urgent for you to decide quickly. The *Wajerumani* (Germans) have already crossed near Voi and wish to attack the Iron Rhino! *Kwaheri* for now."

With this the men dispersed, and the Governor returned to Government house.

Gichuru sat there for quite a while. He was relieved that Gothoro had spoken and quieted the tribesmen. But in his heart, he knew that the white men would never remove the *Kodi* (Tax). He had already seen too much in Meru. His mind was already turning as to what he would do once the war was done. His journey was just beginning!

CHAPTER 21

NJAGE LEAVES MERU (1914)

No one in Meru seemed content with their situation. They were losing their identity day by day and felt helpless. To most Meru's people, it seemed more important than ever to keep their traditions. Groups left for the forest to continue their practices. This was especially true for the Witchmen, whose rites consisted in placing and removing curses, healing, and speaking to the spirits. This too became difficult because of the vigilance of Horne's spies and the missionaries. Horne organized raiding parties into the forests and imprisoned many. Other men left for the settler farms to work on the other side of Mt. Kenya. They worked as laborers, housemen or guards. The Meru family unit was slowly being changed beyond recognition.

Njage saw that Horne and his King were conquering by dividing, and he felt trapped - trapped between causing the end of the well-knit social fabric of the tribe and working with Horne to protect the welfare of his wife, children, and close relatives. He felt his heart being torn apart, but had no answers. Only questions and resignation to the will of Horne.

One day Horne called his men together at Fort Meru and told them that an evil white tribe had declared war on his King. They were the Germans and were already in Maasai land. They had even entered British East Africa near Kilimanjaro. The King had ordered all willing men to help in the fight. Horne told them that if they wished to join as porters or fighters, they should let him know. He also said that soon they might all be forced to join. He gave this a name — *Kuandikisha* (Conscription).

Njage's father, Kithingi, had once told him, "There are many different white tribes. Long ago two white men calling themselves *Wajerumani* (Germans) had passed through Meru in search of a way to climb their mountain, *Kirima Kia Maara*, which the whites now call Mt. Kenya." Also, Njage himself had seen the members of another white tribe, the Waitaliani (Italian) Fathers in the mission down near Thoraka and near Igogi.

Horne told Njage to disseminate these orders among all the people in the various Meru villages. In addition to asking for volunteers for the war, there was the increase in hut tax, and the extension of the *Kitambulisho* (ID card) to the outermost villages. The Meru had been lax in both signing up and carrying it. Each able-bodied man needed to present himself at Fort Meru or other official office with his *Kitambulisho* around his neck or be reissued one. There would be a penalty after that if they did not have it on their person. Gichuru had already warned Njage that all these new measures would come to Meru because these laws had been in place for a while in Gikuyu Land.

Njage swallowed hard. He knew this would not go over well, especially with the old and infirm, who had little way of satisfying this tax. This new directive now clarified his confusion. He knew what he would do. Life was dead for him here.

He would first carry out his duties, and then go to Nairobi to speak with Gichuru. He would try to enlist in the British army. He had seen the KAR when they had marched into Embu. He would see if they would take him. He was still a strong fearless warrior. Yes, this is what he would do!

But first, to his duty. When the people heard what he had to say, there was great rumbling and protest. They yelled and turned their backs to him. He felt like a traitor to his people, friends since childhood. Some men even started burning huts as a protest. Others stated they would go to the forest and not be counted. They clicked their tongues in protest. This seemed the only power they had left!

Njage hung his head and headed home to his wife and family.

"Njuri, I have spoken with Horne and have made my decision."

Njuri looked at him with large eyes.

"What has happened? What decision? You look not yourself - not like yourself at all! So, so sad."

"I have saved enough money for a number of years. I have decided I can no longer work here for Kangangi (Horne). I can no longer face my tribesmen. I can no longer tell them to their face that the King's rules are to be followed when I believe they are so unfair to the tribe. There is no more justice here. Kangangi is asking too much of me."

"Where will you go? What will you do?"

"I have decided to try to join the KAR in Nairobi."

"Njage! There is a war. You might get hurt, even killed. We need you here!"

"Njuri, I do not want to leave you and my children. But I can no longer stomach what I do here."

"E-e-e! I understand. You have been dealing with so much. Our friends are not happy with all the new laws. You must do what you think best. Your sons and daughters can help me. We will survive."

"Call my eldest and then you also remain."

So Njuri went to fetch their eldest, Murungi.

"*Muga*, Murungi. I have much to tell you and Njuri. In a few days I will leave for Nairobi to help in the *Wazungu* (Europeans) war. I have left money to pay for the hut tax and for food. You will have enough. Since you are the eldest, Murungi, my son, you must care for the family. Mostly protect them and follow our traditions. It is difficult, but I know you have much inner strength. I will arrange for you and the older ones to study at the mission school. You need to learn all you can. Your life will be much more complex than ours and you need to learn what the wazungu (foreigners) have to offer."

Murungi looked deeply into Njage's eyes.

"Baba, I will do as you say, but I do not like that you are going so far and into danger!"

"E-e-e," Njuri shook her head in affirmation and continued, "Njage, you must do as you have said. You are strong and a good fighter. As much as I will weep when I think of you so far away, not knowing where, not knowing if you are in danger, I know you do this for us, but also for your peace of mind. As you have said you cannot stay here with Kangangi (Horne) any longer."

Njage took a deep breath. "Njuri, I will miss you. I do not wish to leave you, Kithingi, Muthamia, or the others, but I must. *Murungu* (God) will protect us all."

All three held hands silently for a while, then Njuri spoke, "All will be well. Our ancestral *Nkoma* (Spirits) will protect us. Come now, our daughters have fixed our meal. Let us eat and rejoice while we are still together. Come."

CHAPTER 22

NJAGE AND HORNE (1914)

E arly the next day Njage went to Horne's office at the Fort.

"Bwana Horne, I have decided. I want to fight for the King!"

"O, sorry, Boy, what did you say? Fight? But I need you here. You are my boy! You have been a great help."

"Thank you, Sir, I have tried my best. I like my job, but I am a warrior at heart like you. I need, how you say, 'adventure.'"

"I do understand. I am the same. That's why I came here, far from my own country."

"Please, allow me go to Nairobi. If it pleases you and the commanders, I would like to join the KAR."

"The KAR! It is very difficult to be accepted, but I may be able to help. I can give you a letter to Bwana Colonel Kitchner. He has just come to East Africa to improve the performance of our troops. He is the brother of the great Lord Kitchener, the Secretary of War in Great Britain. I know the man and I know the Colonel will take a liking to you. I hate to lose you, Njage. You have done things well but we must also win this war. We need brave boys like you to fight. Regrettably, I will give you permission. Go now, Boy, and God protect you!"

"*Asante sana*, Sir. I will make you and Meru proud. Please help my sons go to school at the mission."

"I will see that they are educated. All the young must learn English, about God, and the new ways! Come back to us soon. Go now."

"*Kwaheri*. Thank you."

Njage was glad Horne had agreed and that he would look after his family. He felt proud of himself as to how he had managed to turn Horne's mind by comparing Horne's love of adventure to his own. He was beginning to learn how to deal with these foreigners. But, Oh! How he hated to be called Boy! He was a man! A warrior! These small things were beginning to disturb him inordinately. Someday, someday this must end!

CHAPTER 23

NJAGE ARRIVES IN NAIROBI
(late 1914)

As soon as Njage arrived in Nairobi, he tried to find Gichuru. He knew his office was on a place called Victoria Street, but didn't know exactly. After inquiring of a number of strangers, he was led to a clerk's station guard by Somali askaris. They were turbaned and quite tall. Njage had not seen any since he witnessed them marching into Embu when Horne first arrived. He entered the office area and found Gichuru busy with stacks of papers.

"*Hujambo, rafiki.*"

Gichuru looked up from his stacks of papers on his desk, "*Sijambo.* Who is there?" Then looking up, "*Ah, Njage, karibuni* (welcome, come in)! So glad to see you again. I did not expect you so soon. We will feast tonight. I'll send a runner to my wife and children to prepare. You must tell me about Meru."

"There is much to tell, good and bad. But we can talk into the night."

"I knew you might come someday, but this is sudden! You must tell me why! I am really happy to see you, but I think you may have heard of the events on the frontier. Things are moving fast. I will slaughter a goat this evening. Come back at *saa kumi* (4pm) and we will go to my place together."

"E-e-e. Till tonight."

Njage had not been to the capital before. Meru was a distant outpost with a few western-style buildings. He was overwhelmed with the number of people, carriages and horses. There were wide paths and many stone and *mabati* (corrugated iron) buildings. Every once in a while, there was a loud noise like a duck quacking and then a muffled roar. A large carriage without a horse was moving down the street with men and women in large hats and veils. There were places with goods, vegetables, and chickens. Other places with white people eating at tables.

He walked to a large green area with trees and sat with other Africans who were resting in the shade. They were from different tribes and had various appearances. Some slept in the shade. He struck up a conversation with a man who appeared to be a Kamba.

Njage greeted the man, *"Hujambo."*

"Sijambo."

"This is my first time here. It is a very busy place."

"Busy, but a good place to find work. I worked in a white woman's garden for the last few years, but now help is needed in the war. I have decided to join the *Kariakor* (Carrier Corps). We will be porters for the soldiers. I leave in a few days. We are going to *Ngagi Ngai* (Kilimanjaro) to fight the *Wajerumani* (Germans). I like my job with the Memsaab. She just wanted her shamba neatly kept, gave me time to visit my family in Machakos, and I had a small hut on her shamba to share with the cook. It is a good life.

I went to work there when the drought and locusts hit, and we lost our crops. Since we may have to help in the fight anyway, I decided to join the Kariakor. The pay is good. I will miss my family, but what else can we do?"

Njage understood the Kamba man's reasoning. Trying to encourage the man, he said, "It sounds like a good plan. We must all have plans these days. So much change. I am also here to help. I would like to join the KAR."

"O! That is difficult. They only take the best."

"I have a letter from a white man, a D.O. (District Officer) from Fort Meru."

"That will help. Good luck to you!"

Njage fell asleep under a great fig tree until he was awakened by a stream of sunlight hitting his face. He awakened refreshed and happy for the first time in many months. The *Nkoma* (Spirit) near this fig tree must have given him hope and courage. But it was getting late. He must go to Gichuru.

"There you are, Njage! It is just a stone's throw to my place. We go up this road and will be there in about one hour. I am near the forest. I think it will remind you more of Meru. There are hills, not like this flat land here.

As they walked, they spoke of the change, which seemed relentless.

When they arrived, Wanjiku, Gichuru's wife, and his sons and daughters greeted Njage warmly. Njage felt right at home immediately. Gichuru had told his family a lot about his adventures in Meru, and they were very pleased to meet Njage. They knew Njage's family was good to Gichuru.

After the preliminary conversation, Njage started to explain his arrival, "I see many new and different things here at the capital. Things I did not know existed! Each day brings to us more adjustments and unhappiness in Meru."

"Tell me, *rafiki* (my friend). We are being ruled and we have little say about how. More whites and East Indians arrive. Now with this war, there are soldiers from many different white tribes. The hut tax is causing anger. Registration and the *Kitambulisho* (I.D.) are causing many to be depressed. Many do not want to fight these white men's battles. Some go to Maasai land to blend in, since the Maasai have outright refused to register. In many ways they are much braver than we are. What do you think Laikisat will do?"

"Yes, this is what caused me to leave and come here. I feel unwanted among my people. I am tired of being a white mouthpiece. I have not seen Laikisat for some time and don't know his thoughts yet."

"*Rafiki*, my heart is as heavy as yours. But if we do not do it, they will find others, and some of our tribesmen will be harsher with the people."

"So, I too must register and carry the *Kitambulisho* (I.D.)! Now there will be punishments for not having it around my neck as you warned me! As if I do not know who I am! I am Njage Muriuki, husband of Njuri, a athaka (warrior) of the Murungi Age-Set. I am proud and brave. But now I must carry a sign, like the stamp we put on our cattle!"

"Njage, Bwana, *rafiki*! We do this for our families! I have given all of this much thought. There are other men here who are also planning for the future. The war has gotten in the way. Someday you will meet them. We will talk and plan together, patiently.

The Wazungu (Europeans) are impatient people. They
will tire. This is our land, and these are our people. We will
meet and plan after this wartime passes. Most importantly
we must remain united — the three of us. Laikisat, you
and I, always!

"So now tell me why have you come? Though I am
enjoying seeing and talking with you, I am sure you have
other reasons than to visit with a friend. I know what a
long and difficult journey it is from the other side of the
Kirinyaga (Mt. Kenya)."

"Yes. It was a difficult journey. I wanted to see you,
because I always feel more confident after our visits. I,
too, have a plan. I am tired of giving Horne's orders to my
people and seeing their unhappiness. I now have found a
way to get away from Horne and the other British in Meru.
I am still strong and want adventure. I will help with this
Wazungu (European's) war."

"It is good to decide. One always feels better after
making a decision. My position here is fairly secure. I am
working with the Governor, who at first did not want
war. But the generals now have orders from London. I
do paperwork for them. They are pleased with my work."

"I have a letter from Horne to Kitchner to join the KAR.
I hope I will be successful."

"Good! They are looking for recruits. It will be sometime
before the Indian Expeditionary Force will arrive. There
have been preparations and war games to prepare to go to
Ngagi Ngai (Kilimanjaro) at the border. They are planning
to send men."

"I will go tomorrow with my letter."

"It is good to go soon. If you do not go soon, they may
force you, and then you will not know where they might

assign you. They call this *Kuandikisha* (*Conscription*). It is like slavery, but they will pay you a pittance, especially if they put you in the *Kariakor*, porters for the British."

"Yes. Horne also used the word *Kuandikisha* (Conscription). I met a Kamba today who has joined the *Kariakor*. I would prefer to be a warrior and fight like a man. I want to have weapons and learn how to use them to defend myself - I am an *Il-murran* (warrior), like Laikisat!"

"Yes, I also, but I am a bit older and they tell me they need me here. You are very eligible because of your height and build. You are tall, strong, and agile from the Meru hills. The KAR is looking for men like you. I will introduce you to General Kitchner tomorrow. His office is in the building next to mine. I will tell him we worked together with Horne. Now sit here. My wife, Wanjiku is preparing ugali, sukuma wiki, and irio. My eldest son has killed a goat and has begun roasting it. We will feast and enjoy tonight! No worries about the future. Tonight is in the hands of our ancestors."

"So very glad to see you again, *Ndugu* (Brother)!"

CHAPTER 24

LAIKISAT MEETS LORD DELAMARE (late 1914)

That same year, not long after the short rains were subsiding, Laikisat began to notice many foreigners moving down the Great Rift Valley toward the Kilimanjaro. This disturbed him for Kilimanjaro, *Ngagi Ngai* was the home of God. There were large caravans of Africans: Swahili, Kamba and others moving goods unloaded from the Iron Rhino. The *Wazungu* (Europeans) had many rifles.

The elders, but also Gichuru, had told him that the white tribe called Germans were fighting against the whites, or British, whom he had seen in Nairobi. They were the same ones who had made Gichuru Chief of Chiefs of the Gikuyu. The Germans were entrenched on the other side of the Kilimanjaro and had already ventured into British territory. Laikisat had known about this German tribe. They were in the southern part of Maasai land. The Maasai there called them the *Deutchi*.

Laikisat sat and watched the caravan's approach. One day a foreigner was seen not far from his *manyatta* (Maasai compound) together with many *murran* (warriors). As he stared, he seemed to recognize one of the warriors. He walked toward this man, whom he recognized as his friend Koinet.

"Koinet, *Suba*! I wish to join you warriors. Can you intercede with the Bwana for me?"

"You should ask him yourself. He respects outspoken men with courage. He is a great man among the British. They call him *Lordi D* (Lord Delamare). *Lordi* means he has much power among the wazungu. Approach him respectfully and ask. He knows Kiswahili but also some Maasai. Speak to him in Maasai first and then tell him of your adventures."

Koinet explained that they were from the area known as Narok as far as Naivasha. The murran told Laikisat that this Lord respected the Maasai. He even sometimes behaved as a murran! He gave them rides in his wheeled horseless carriage and even had invited some to his house to sit by the fire where they shared tales of their exploits. Lord Delamare was a great leader and fighter. He had fought with the Somalis in their land. In his early days he had trekked from Somalia through Meru to the Great Rift. He had interceded with the Governors for the Maasai to keep land for grazing their cattle. This was difficult for Delamare, because so many whites were crawling like locusts over the highlands taking the good land for themselves. Delamare fought to have the Maasai continue their nomadic ways provided they kept to certain designated lands. He had persuaded the Maasai that the Germans would be worse task masters than the British. The murran agreed to patrol the border with him on the near side of the great Kilimanjaro.

So Laikisat became informed of the news in this part of Maasai land and was grateful to Koinet.

"Thank you, Koinet! I will go now."

Laikisat had not been as excited since he had traveled to Nairobi for the first time. He wondered to himself, *could it be possible for me to join the Lord's murran? I must ask. I hope it can be so!"*

Laikisat traveled the short distance to the Lord's camp to speak with him. Laikisat had had his impressive head of hair braided that very morning. He spent hours with his brothers by the stream grooming and painting ocher on his face and shoulders. He was naked except for the dark, red blanket thrown over his shoulder, falling past his waist. He had large carved ivory earrings and carried a large spear and buffalo hide shield. He walked upright with a spring in his step. To the outside world he strode as a noble pharaoh.

Approaching Delamare's camp, Laikisat greeted him. "Suba, Lordi D! I am known as Laikisat. I am a warrior of my clan. I have come to beg a favor."

"*Suba, Murran. Habari ya leo?* What news of today?"

"I have come with these warriors who have agreed to patrol the frontier. We must stop the *Wajerumani* (Germans) take-over of our land. They are not to be trusted."

" We are fighting an even greater battle in my homeland, Great Britain, against this *Wajerumani* tribe. If they get control, your land will not be safe.

"I have come to ask if I can join you."

"Tell me why you think you want this?"

"I like adventure. I have already been to Nairobi to trade with my friend Gichuru. I have travelled as far as Mutindwa on the other side of *Kirinyaga* (Mt. Kenya). I have seen many things and many changes. I killed a lion when I entered the il-murran. I do not have fear. I also have learned some Kiswahili."

"I respect that you have been so forthright with me. We need all the brave men we can get. So far, we *Wazungu* (Europeans) are few. More may come. But the time now is short. I promise if you join us, I will work hard for your clan to remain in this region. You need to swear to follow my orders and not shoot or throw your spear unless directed. I will give you a rifle later and show you its use. I like your way of life. It is free. Join the others in the morning and we will begin our safari south. I see you know Koinet. I will tell Koinet to teach you."

"*Asante,* Bwana. You will not be sorry."

"*Tutaonana.* See you."

And so, he took his leave for the night. It was in this way Laikisat first met the great Lord Delamare. In the days that followed they came to know and respect each other and their respective cultures. Laikisat began to think of this Lord as a king. In the years to come, Delamare was to play an influential role in this land's history. Laikisat was glad to have been accepted into this band of warriors. With this he now entered into white man's history.

BOOK 4:

LOVE AND SLAVERY

Awakening

First a sole voice from the arabesque
Called into the darkness
Then the first 'twas pierced by a nail
A responding wail,
A clashing hail.

And then the two in contradiction
Yet in rhyme
Removed the blackness
And the dark
And met the sun!

At dawn on the East African coast waking before dawn to the call of the *muezzins'* calls for prayer from the surrounding mosques.

CHAPTER 25

OMARI AND MAHIRI
(Early 1700)

The slave caravan slowly made its way back to Lamu. Mahiri had thought Omari's looks were very exotic and she liked him from first they met. In the few days since their marriage she began to appreciate his kindness and his care for her.

Now they had begun their long safari to Omari's home on the coast. They descended from Mutindwa following the rivers until they flowed into the great Tana. The land became dry scrub except for the lush bank of the river, which was a torrent from the recent rains. Now Mt. Kenya was at their back in all its majesty. It had filled the entire horizon, but slowly, day by day, it sank until it disappeared completely. Mahiri's eyes were filled with scenes so different than the forests and fields of her home in Meru.

"Omari, my eyes are saddened. My homeland is disappearing! All I have ever known - my parents, sisters - all gone forever!"

"Oh, Mahiri! Do not be sorrowful. Hopefully our love

for each other will replace your sadness and you will always have your memories of the mountain. Come, see the gazelles running freely! You too now are entering a different life - free of the old rules of your tribe."

"Yes, but there will be new rules. Women always have more rules than men, and I am fearful of what is to come."

As they descended into the plains, she was both frightened and awed by the abundance of life, the enormous herds of antelope, zebra, the enormity and playfulness of elephant, and the terrifying roars of the lion. She kept close to Omari, day and night. She needed his assurance and protection. He was more and more pleased with his new companion. The desert scrubland was hotter than she had ever experienced, and the only reprieve was the river. The many cruel insects gave the caravan members little relief. However, Mahiri enjoyed the extended time together with Omari, and their mutual love grew. Their physical attraction blossomed into strong companionship.

Even though the rains had been over for three weeks, the river appeared wide and the flow was rapid. In some places it had overflowed the banks. At Golbanti they saw Galla tribesmen and Maasai. The Galla travelled by camel carrying their houses on the backs of the beasts. Their cattle and goats followed them.

In the town they saw a place where a river dhow was anchored. Up to this time Mahiri had only seen river craft, hollowed-out tree trunks, navigating small streams. But this was a true wonder. It was a large craft made of wood with tall wooden polls. Tied to wooden cross polls were large pieces of cloth tied in bundles. Omari told her these would be unfurled to catch the wind and propel the dhow forward. He told her the dhow would take them the final leg of the safari to Lamu. Mahiri was glad that they could stop walking. Lately she was feeling more and more tired, and not herself.

They camped for a few days while preparations for the final leg of the journey were made ready. The slaves were hauled down into the lower part of the dhow and their ankles secured between two large trunks from trees that had holes for their ankles. Two large Arabs kept watch, their whips always at the ready. Mahiri cringed at this. She had never witnessed this kind of cruelty in her village, and she wondered about what her new life would be like, but Omari reassured her that at his home, things would be different.

"I am afraid of these men"

"Mahiri, do not be alarmed. My father and I can protect you. You are my wife and no one will question that."

"I wish to be a good wife."

"I too do not like slavery. My father and I are only traders of goods, but in order to secure these, we must go with the caravan. It is very lucrative for these Arabs. Some of these slaves will go to coastal plantations to care for rice and millet. Others are shipped to far off places. We, ourselves, have nothing to do with that."

"But just being here with these evil *Warabu* (Arab) men gives them assurance that they can continue with treating men worse than animals."

"What would you have us do? To protest would enflame the slave traders to do us harm or enslave or beat us. In this way they leave our settlements to us, and we can rule ourselves."

Mahiri fell into deep thought for quite a while.

Changing the subject, she began, "Do you know that

our Meru elders tell us that long ago we lived near here on a place surrounded by water, and that we had to leave because evil men wanted to rule and control us. They called the place Mbwaa (present day Manda Island). We left in groups and headed back along this same River Tana. We roamed for a long time, until fairly recently we found *Kirinyaga* (Mt. Kenya). The great Mountain has been our protection."

"I did not know. But I do know that many of the tribes here in our villages came from inland. So now you return to your forefathers' spirits! It is all predestined by Allah!"

"I am glad to have you and I think we may not be alone."

"What do you mean? Here we stand alone by the river, just two..."

"You know, I don't feel like myself - I think - I think-there may be a third here," pointing to her belly.

'Praise Allah! What great news! My family will be honored, and I am overjoyed"

All was now ready, and they set sail down the river for a night and a day. Mahiri was amazed at the size of the unfurled sails and how the wind filled them so full!

That evening they reached the enormous delta of the river and the ship began to rock to and fro. Mahiri became sick and frightened. Hundreds of rivulets flowed toward a large water in the distance. But the knowledgeable captain steered the boat safely ahead until, to her awestruck eyes, Mahiri saw the largest body of water she had ever seen! It stretched from horizon to horizon and the waves were enormous. As the water hit her face, she tasted salt! This is what the elders sang about. The great saltwater where they once lived before the escape from the men who came on the houses that floated on water. She was completing a cycle in her tribe's history.

The dhow hugged the coast until they entered an estuary and soon some huts became visible on a distant island. Mahiri was amazed to see some very tall houses. All were clustered very close to each other. She wondered to herself, "Where did they plant their crops? Even the ground was covered in stone!" Also, the place was full of people scurrying too and fro. There were many small boats and large dhows sitting offshore. People were jumping on and off the dhows and the smaller boats, off and onto the shore. Others were carrying all sorts of goods: large mangrove polls, baskets of rock, and fresh fish from the sea. There were baskets of vegetables and fruits being loaded and unloaded from the boats. Mahiri's mouth remained wide open as her amazement grew at this scene of abundance unfolding before her.

Mahiri had never seen so many different types of people. She had seen the *Warabu* (Arabs) and the Swahili in the caravan, but they were mostly men. Now she saw men dressed in clean white robes wearing *kofia* (interesting round hats). She saw a variety of people of differing skin tones: black, brown, and some almost white! Shirtless men walked or worked by the sea. They wore colorful *kikois* (lengths of cloth) wrapped around the waist.

Then she started to see the women further away. Some women were covered head to toe with a black covering, only their eyes visible. Omari told her these garments were called *buibui.*

Though this word meant *spider,* the garments were the proper outdoor covering for the women of Lamu. Mahiri thought, *I knew deep in my heart that I would be exchanging one set of rules for others. Rules were always stricter for our sex!*

Other women had very colorful long dresses with colorful head scarves. Still others were bare headed women draped in an overabundance of long colorful fabrics. Many had a colorful dot of color on their forehead.

Mahiri felt so out of place in her brown cloth wrapped over her shoulder, her breasts covered only by green beads.

Finally, she saw some women who looked somewhat like her, in just ordinary brown covering, but working very hard cleaning the streets or carrying objects on their heads. They looked tired and unhappy.

Then, close to a very large house with columns, she saw two of the strangest looking creatures of them all! A man in a tall rounded black hat with a big brim stood in the doorway. He had white cloth tightly wrapped around each leg and wore very tall black leather shoes. His torso was also tightly covered in white fabric with many silver buttons glistening in the sun. His face was as white as the fruit of the Baobab, so white, he looked ill.

Next to him stood a woman. The woman, Mahiri supposed his woman, looked huge. Even though she had a tiny waist, her dress from the waist down stuck out very far. Mahiri could not see her feet! There was more cloth draped around her top and she wore the largest hat Mahiri had ever seen. It was decorated with ribbon and feathers. Mahiri thought it was like what a Witchman might wear to a cursing ritual! The woman's head was also shaded by a small cloth roof supported by a stick she held in her hand.

The Baobab-fruit-faced man and the woman slowly walked down the stairs to the street. They walked arm in arm to the waterfront! Mahiri had never seen this before! Arm-in-arm! Mahiri had been taught that it was proper for the woman to walk ten paces behind the man, but arm-in-arm was highly improper. Even the other males and females on this island walked separately. Only these milky-white people walked like this!

Omari woke Mahiri from her amazed staring by calling out. "Mahiri, we are approaching the dock and are very close to my home. *Karibu* to Lamu. Welcome. I hope you will feel at home. My family awaits us!"

"Omari, everything I have seen so far amazes me. I did not expect so many differences! I feel different and out of place even in my clothes. I am afraid I will not be accepted. I hope I can fulfill your wishes"

"Do not fear, my mother is a good woman who will guide you in dress and in our ways. She is kind and welcoming. And when she knows you like I do; she will call you her daughter."

And so, they disembarked and walked a few hundred feet up a small street. On the way they passed a large open space with an enormous building facing them. As they walked by they heard cries and laments from within the building. As Mahiri and Omari passed near the building they saw faces behind bars placed across small holes in the walls. They were being held in subterranean caves.

"Omari! I have never seen such a place! How horrid!"

"This is the prison where murderers and violent robbers are kept. They have committed crimes and need to be punished. You will get used to it."

"*Mungu,* save me!"

Omari tried to change the subject. "This open space is where there is a market each morning. You will see."

They now turned and went up another small alley, which wound uphill to a large three-story building. There were many houses on each side of the street, one up against the other. There was only a small alleyway between houses on each side. Mahiri felt very hot, but at least the high buildings provided shade and there was a cool breeze that came up the street from the harbor that dried her sweat.

"This is my home. We will live here with my family. *Karibu,* welcome, welcome."

"Oh! How different this house is from anything I have ever known!"

"Let us enter. My family awaits above."

They entered through two huge carved wooden doors that creaked and sang as if they were objecting. Inside there was a lovely open space with a pool where a jet of water from a pipe rose and fell. It was making small ripples in the water held in a large basin at the bottom. Around the edges were pots with flowering plants and small trees with strange hanging fruits. She was told that one was a pawpaw tree at one end, and at the other end, a large avocado tree.

A staircase at the end opposite the entrance led up, and as she looked up, there were open spaces where people could sit. Many doors led from the balustraded walkway opening into shadowed peaceful rooms. Omari led her up one staircase, then around to another, until they had gone up three flights.

When they reached the top they were outside again, but very high above the town. There was a canopy on one end where three people sat on large cushions and dressed in very fine clothes. The vista was amazing — the sea, islands, and coconut trees! Up here was a light, pleasant breeze, unlike the heat of the street below.

"*Karibuni,* welcome Omari! And is this your wife the porters have told us about?"

"Yes, Father, we are so glad to finally have arrived. The

journey was very hard, but I have brought you many riches to trade. And my biggest prize is here: Mahiri from the Meru tribe. I have found my love and there is another prize within her! I will present her formally to you tonight after we have washed."

"Mahiri stared at the lovely woman who approached her. She was in a black robe, but you could see the colorful dress she had on beneath and the gold and silver jewelry. Her uncovered face was a deep chocolate."

"This is my mother, Fahtma."

"O my son! My dear Omari! Praise be to Allah! We will have a grandchild! What happiness you bring to us old *wazee* (elders)! We had heard that she was a beautiful Ameru, but, I must say, she is lovelier than there are words. Come my child, Mahiri, you must be tired. To be with child on a long journey is very difficult. You must be very strong to have weathered the safari. I will take you to bathe and relax. My maids will rub you with oil and fine spices, so you will be even more alluring to your Omari! *Bis bi lie!* You are very beautiful! Do you understand my speech?"

Mahiri stared at the beautiful women, and hesitated, but then gathered her words. "O yes. My father insisted I learn Kiswahili, but I find some of your words different."

Fahtma was overjoyed that she could understand.

"You will learn. Our *Kiamu* (Lamu dialect) is somewhat different, but it is the best Kiswahili. Over many years, poets have written beautiful verses in our *Kiamu*. You will see. Come now."

She took Mahiri down the stairs to a small room with a large basin carved of stone. There was also a large stone table on one side. The maid scurried in and turned a lever on a pipe, and clean cool water flowed into the basin.

Omari's mother, Fahtma. told Mahiri to disrobe and enter the basin. She then told the maids what to do, and left Mahiri to their care. Mahiri finally relaxed as they washed her, then placed her on the table and rubbed her with coconut oil and spices she had never smelled before. It was like a dream! The servants told Mahiri to rest while they gathered her new clothes. That evening she would be formally presented to the family at dinner. Her skin had never felt so soft, nor had it ever glistened like the black opal stones on the mountain.

Upstairs Omari and his father, Sharif, discussed the terms of the trade for the goods that Omari had procured and how they were to be dispersed among the town merchants. Some of the goods might earn more from the traders on the dhows that were headed to Yemen, Persia or India. His father was very pleased.

And so began Mahiri's new life in a city that had already existed a thousand years and had seen many different people come and go. She was apprehensive, but no longer afraid. It seemed Omari's mother was very kind and would teach her new ways. She could be happy here.

At dinner Mahiri was introduced formally to the men of the family: Omari's father, Sharif, and his older brother, Mohammed. They were seated with the other men on large pillows on the rooftop while slaves served them food. Sharif was very cordial and welcomed Mahiri and asked her questions about her home and safari. Mohammed, however, did not speak and seemed to have a permanent scowl on his face. It seemed to Mahiri that Mohammed wished to be somewhere else.

Mahiri and Omari's mother, Fahtma, then withdrew to another area of the rooftop, where a number of women were sitting. They all sat reclining on large soft pillows to enjoy the evening meal while a soft breeze blew over them. She learned that this was the extended family, grandmother, aunts, and others.

After dinner Fahtma led Mahiri to a room on the second story with a very large open doorway facing the courtyard, and high narrow windows on the street side. Thus, the room caught the cool sea breeze. A gossamer curtain danced over the large high wooden bed. She climbed into this luxurious cocoon and immediately fell into a deep sleep dreaming of her new life.

After she had rested for quite a while, she heard Omari enter. He had also bathed and was wearing only his bright white *kikoi*, a cloth wrapped at the waist. He looked to her like a spirit warrior out of her dream. For a moment she did not know whether she was in this world or had passed to the next. When he saw her lying on the bed clothed only in a soft silk, he could see her glistening black body.

"O! Mahiri! You are *Malaika*, my *Malaika!*"

"Omari, I may be your *angel*, but you are descended from the White Cloud of *Kirinyaga*! Come join me in my gossamer nest!"

He was overwhelmed and his love and desire were heightened. Their love making that evening confirmed to both of them that they had made the right choice.

CHAPTER 26

SAFARI KIDOGO
Small Safari (Early 1700)

Mahiri and Omari had now been together for a few years. Their first son, Akili, was born healthy and strong, and a second child, a girl, about two years later. They still happily lived in the family home.

On one of those perfect equatorial days when the sea breeze was gently blowing, Omari decided that it was a perfect day to take Mahiri on a short dhow safari. She had recovered from the second birth and he wanted to show his appreciation and love. The two of them boarded a small dhow and went up the Lamu channel to Jipi creek. They took two slaves who were in charge of carrying and preparing food. Omari was an experienced sailor and only relied on the men when he needed to lower or raise the sail or when they were ready to dock. They had a large supply of fresh coconuts stored below deck which they could use for fresh water when they were thirsty. There was nothing like the refreshing coconut on a hot day!

"Omari! Asante! What a lovely day to be on the sea!

It is so much cooler than in the hot rooms of the house."

"Yes, these are the best times. One feels alive on the sea! We are going to a place that I know of to find some ducks for the Maulidi feast."

Mahiri had been instructed in the Moslem faith by Fahtma and the other elder ladies in the household. She found that Allah and the *Murungu* of the Meru shared many qualities. She enjoyed most of the stories from the Koran. She especially liked those of how justice triumphed over cruelty and oppression. Another favorite was the story of Musa, the prophet, who led the Israelites. Allah divided the sea so they could pass to freedom away from the evil pharaoh. It was so similar to the Meru escape from Mbwaa, the island where her tribe once lived. They were saved by Murungu just like the people in the Koran. She was really feeling that *Murungu, Mungu,* or Allah, were smiling on her, Omari, and the new lives she had brought into this world.

They soon reached a swampy area that had many mangrove trees. They disembarked and walked a mile or so to a small camp that Omar's family had set up some time ago. There was a pond nearby where many different birds came to drink and swim.

Omari pointed at the pond, "See how many ducks come here. Look at that fat one! Later we will catch a few to take home until the feast day."

"This is a nice place to spend the day and night! Thank you for bringing me here. I also see some cashew trees and the fruit are ready! I have really come to love these nuts! We have nothing like them in Meru. I will pick some and when the fire is lit, I will roast some to add to our rice."

Omari smiled. "*Asante.* That will be a welcome addition."

Suddenly, a huge clap of thunder echoed all around, and the sky darkened.

"Mahiri, grab your things and let's run to the small hut where we will stay."

He pointed into the distance where Mahiri could barely see the roof of a building. They began running when the heavens opened, and the torrential rain and wind fell hard and quick. Mahiri could hardly see in front of her. But she spied a small shed just a few paces from where she was and began running to it."

"Mahiri, stop, stop! Not that way!"

But before he could stop her, she was already inside the dry hut and was shaking off the rain. She looked around and saw four huge tree logs. She sat on one and removed her sandals. She was tired from the run and was glad to find a resting place so close. As she caught her breath she began wondering about this place.

Where she sat reminded her of the logs on the dhow. The two huge logs were hinged at one end and had a large metal hasp at the other. Every few feet there where holes cut in the logs, large enough for an arm or a leg. There was dried blood on some walls and some fresh blood on the logs. She jumped up! Realizing where she was, and she began trembling.

At that point Omari and the two slaves arrived. The slaves remained outside where there were benches covered by a thatched overhang. They seemed reluctant to enter.

Mahiri could hardly form her words. "Omari, what is this place? My Meru intuition tells me that there are evil *Nkoma* (spirits) here, what you call *Shetani* (Satan). Is that why you wanted me not to come this way? So, I would not see the results of evil?"

"I was wanting to keep you from knowing this place - it is a bad place. It belongs to the slave traders. It is a far distance from the city, and it is close to the creek where their dhows can dock. As you now have guessed it is part of my brother Mohammed's work. He allows the slavers to come on our trading safaris and has given them this place to keep the slaves until the ships arrive. Remember on our long journey here there were many Bantus and members of other tribes who were chained?"

"Yes, I remember being very disturbed. It sickened me!"

"These logs are to keep them secure until the ship arrives. The holes are for their ankles. When the heavy log is placed on top, the hasp is locked, and they cannot run."

"How long are they kept here in this prison?"

"One man is set to watch them until they can be put on the ship. Sometimes a week, sometimes a few months."

"Months! It is so cruel! Are they like wild animals? This is not right! Are they fed? How do they wash? Terrible, terrible. I cannot bear it. This is why my people left Mbwaa! My people must have seen others taken in this way! So, this is why we escaped across the channel and journeyed for so many years. Now I understand! They were escaping this horrible end. Omari take me from here. And the fresh blood? It may be from poor men and women who were here just a few days before we arrived! And the dried blood from those that we travelled with years ago! And this is why your two slaves do not wish to enter! Allah have mercy!"

"Mahiri, please don't. We will go to the hut now. The sea captains take them to many places - Persia, Yemen, India - across the salt sea. If they did not keep them here, they would find other places and other traders to guard them. This is only a minor place. In Zanzibar, further south, there is a huge slave market where many thousands are bought and sold. They are kept in a vile dungeon before they are put on a ship. They must wait for the favorable monsoon to change direction so they may travel east."

"I knew about slaves. I thought they would be like our cooks and maids, who go about town freely, eat our food, and do what we request. Fahtma is very kind to them. But this is different. This is inhuman. And Mohammed is part of this. I understand his scowl now! His wealth and part of ours earned from this! This cruel treatment of humanity! It must stop!"

"Our slaves are treated well as are most in Lamu. Some gain their freedom and some women even marry our men and are treated the same as Swahili wives."

"But each log has 40 holes - 40 bodies crammed here for days. I cannot imagine. O Allah have mercy. Take me away from here!"

"Yes, let's go and do not think on this anymore. I don't like this either and when and if I ever can do anything about this I will, but I fear my brother, Mohammed. As first born he will inherit the running of the entire trade. He has many friends among the important people in Lamu. He is easily impressed by power and wealth. We are very different."

"Omari, I know you are kind. Forgive my reaction, but I am upset. Some of these people could be, could have been, my tribesman, my relatives."

"I realize this is difficult, and that is why I tried keeping you from seeing it. There are many evil things in this world I cannot change; many things in Allah's will that I cannot control."

"I am not blaming you. I know in my village there were

things I saw: cattle raids, the beating of women by cruel men, and the Masai and others that caused us so much fear. All I know is that none of this is of Allah, or *Murungu*! It is of whom you call *Shetani*, or we call the evil *Nkoma*!"

"Right now, I must respect my father. This is our culture. If I would go against this I would be banished from my family. My brother would see that evil came to us. He is not a good man. We all would suffer. I cannot question that which is."

"I realize there are limits to what you can do. You are the youngest. Some day, though, this must end. Maybe when Sharif is in paradise and Mohamed meets his end, then change will come. You must do what you can at that time. Promise me. Someday all peoples must be free!"

"I promise. Let us go. The rain has slowed, and the men must build a fire before it gets dark."

BOOK 5:

WAR 2

CHAPTER 27

NJAGE GOES TO WAR (1914-15)

Njage had told Horne he wanted to help fight the war. Arriving in Nairobi he spent a few days with Gichuru who spoke with Colonel H.E.C. Kitchner who introduced Njage to commander Jollie of the KAR. Njage was tall for a Meru. When Jollie saw him he immediately took to him, both for his physique as well as his command of Kiswahili. Though his English was only fair, Jollie felt he would be an asset to the group. He also liked that Gichuru knew Njage well and trusted Njage because of their work together in Meru.

Recruits were needed badly, and many were not the best. Jollie assigned Njage to a group of Somalis who would train him to shoot, march, and drill. Njage rapidly gained their respect because he was already a great archer and spearman, and he translated his skill to the rifle. It was only the recoil that he needed to get used to.

Njage was proud of how he looked in new khaki shorts and his large brimmed hat, which was the new uniform of the KAR. Carrying a rifle and knife on his belt made him feel like a warrior again. Though different from his earlier life as a Meru *athaka* (warriors), he again felt like adventure would find him and it soon did.

In a matter of weeks, they were prepared to travel toward the coast to counter the attack of the Germans under the infamous General Paul von Lettow-Vorbeck, known as the African Kaiser. Even Njage had heard of this very fearsome General. He commanded his tribe, plus many African Askari from near Kilimanjaro. He had more than thirty-thousand riflemen and eight-thousand native troops on the east side of the mountain in Tanganyika.

Njage and his troop of KAR boarded the Iron Rhino and headed for Voi. This was an amazing thrill for Njage who had only walked all his life. As they travelled, he saw huge herds of elephant and zebra. During the night they could hear lions roar and even saw a few prides on the prowl in the moonlight. Some of the men recalled stories from their fathers who had worked on laying the tracks. They told of the many men attacked and killed by the "man eaters of Tsavo," the lions that would attack and devour workers during the night. Others recalled that some men even referred to the Iron Rhino as the "Lunatic Express!"[12]

The men felt confident and prepared for the conflict. Njage felt well trained as a member of the 3rd KAR. He even had been promoted to sergeant of the Bantu contingent. The colonel noticed he was an excellent marksman and leader. Njage gave credit to his training as a Meru warrior, to the instruction of Horne, and to the Somali's who had trained him in Nairobi. He tried to transfer this training to his men.

There were one-hundred and eighty-thousand men in the *Kariakor*. A large number of these were to meet Njage's contingent and the others at Voi. There they would go their

separate ways according to the master plan. Each man in
the Kariakor carried fifty pounds of food and equipment,
but each was entitled to only one-half cup of cooked *posho*
(porridge) per day. Njage wondered how the Kamba man
he met in Nairobi was faring, and was glad that he, himself,
was in the KAR instead of the *Kariakor*.

The plan, once at Voi, was that one diversionary prong
was to head to Longido on the west side of Mt. Kilimanjaro.
The main prong was to head toward Taveta on the East
side of that mountain. The two would hopefully meet in a
pincer movement at Taveta and hopefully move to Tanga
on the coast as a single unit. The *Wajerumani* (Germans)
had been entrenched in this part of British East Africa since
the very start of the war in early 1914 by the legendary
African Kaiser.

At Voi Njage's contingent joined other soldiers from
many places. Each day Njage learned something more
about the white men and their different tribes. He also
found out more about African tribes from other regions as
far as Nyasaland. He even met Kashmiris, Bengalis, South
Africans, Australians, and Scotsmen. There were mounted
regiments, hundreds of porters, the KAR, the Scouts, and
the East African Mounted Rifles. All to converge on Taveta
in British East Africa and retake the town for the King.
Seeing this mass of men and equipment, Njage now finally
understood the reach and power of the British Empire. He
realized what a small cog East Africa was in the Empire!

Once arriving in Voi, Njage and his battalion trekked for
days toward Longido, a settlement and camp on a hill to the
west of Kilimanjaro. Finally arriving near Longido hill, they
found it obscured in mist, but very well fortified. Njage's
contingent fought bravely in this skirmish. However, they

could not break through to take this position and had to retreat because the Kariakor had not reached them in time. The men could not sustain the attack mostly for lack of fresh water. They retreated back to Namanga. Though the group suffered many casualties, Njage managed to come out unharmed. Njage wished that the Kariakor had been better organized to provide the supplies they desperately needed.

The Germans remained entrenched in northern German East Africa (Tanganyika) and in Taveta in British East Africa (Kenya). The British troops themselves even were defeated in the Battle of Tanga on the coast. The greatest Empire in the world had succumbed to *Wajerumani* (*German*) guerrilla tactics that the African Kaiser had learned in the best military school in Europe.[13]

Njage's mind was like a sponge. He spotted this strategy immediately. His thoughts, though, were about the future. How could he use these successful tactics? He would try to incorporate these guerrilla tactics into the training of his troops. For a moment he also let his mind wander into a dangerous chasm: might he use these tactics someday to free his people. He stored it all away for now people?

They fought in small skirmishes first on the west side of Kilimanjaro, and then on the east, but mostly trekked for months. Through 1915 and well into the next year, they took small towns, and had to retreat from others. Eventually they began the trek to Morogoro, on the German Railroad close to Dar Es Salaam.

On the way the rains began, and the way became impassible. Wagons and mules became stuck in the sticky black cotton soil and soldiers lost shoes and boots as they tried to pull their feet from the thick, slippery, black-cotton soil. Insect bites and foul water caused infections. There were shortages of food and water. The troops became exhausted. It was the worst journey that Njage had ever experienced.

Njage also noted that there were many more insects here in this part of German East Africa than in Meru. The numerous insects from the swamp and damp soil burrowed into the skin and caused powerful sores. The fetid swamps were the insects' perfect habitat. The streams in Meru were clean and clear. Here the pools of water were undrinkable. Many men became sick; many, died. The numerous Malarial mosquitos were a persistent problem. Unused to tropical diseases, European soldiers especially were most vulnerable. Quinine was effective in preventing and curing malaria, but the medicine was in limited supply.

Besides malaria, there was the problem of the wounded men from their skirmishes. They needed medical attention and had to trek or be carried back to safe camps. This was not always possible and led to further fatalities. In one skirmish near Salaita Hill, Njage received a glancing blow from a bullet to his leg. Treating the wounds required significant time to recover his ability to walk. Njage was fortunate to be near the camp to be able to rest during recuperation.

While recuperating in Voi, Njage used this time to perfect his ideas of how to train his men. He especially thought about the guerrilla tactics of the African Kaiser's men at Tanga. They were so much more effective than the British tactics. He saw right through the incompetence of the British generals and commanders. Once recovered he would teach his troops the better tactics. He had the confidence that they could be taught to win.

Njage also had an uncanny expertise in tracking. He was able to lead through uncharted and difficult landscapes. This ability attracted the attention of General Smuts who now was in command. The General, a South African who had fought against the British in the Boar War, now was put in command of all of British East Africa. Smuts was welcomed by the colonials because they were desperate for competent leadership.[14] For almost three years the British were mired down by the African Kaiser.

Once Smuts realized Njage's abilities, he elevated Njage's rank, adding troop tracker training to his responsibilities. By 1917 Njage was one of the few Africans who had survived in his contingent of the KAR. He sustained wounds but recovered quickly. He seemed indifferent to pain.

Once fully recovered he helped scout and lead the men to recapture the towns the Germans had taken. By this time the British fleet was on the coast, and most of the *Wajerumani* were retreating south and west as far as Portuguese territory. Njage and the men finally made it to Tanga which had fallen to British naval bombardment. Now Britain controlled the entire northern railway in German East Africa.

Finally arriving at Tanga on the coast, Njage suffered another setback from a severe fever. Many men were falling ill; some, even died. Later it was identified as influenza, a highly contagious disease which was to engulf the world for the next two years. It has been estimated that five-hundred million people became infected world-wide and over fifty million died.[15] One third of the world's population had succumbed to this awful pandemic. East Africa was not spared. It was to cause much death and suffering in the following few years. Once again Njage beat the odds and recovered.

Since the war was winding down, Njage now received new orders. He was to accompany the Somalis back home to northern East Africa.

Among the men were a number of Somali wounded. Upon arrival, Njage was to see that they were paid and discharged. The government office on the island of Lamu would be notified by wireless and the money would be waiting for them. They were to board a ship in Dar Es Salam, travel to Lamu and then transfer to other dhows heading for British Somalia. Njage could then begin his long safari home to Meru.

He was overwhelmed at the request. It was a great responsibility to be entrusted with this honor. He was so excited and thankful that finally the fighting was over, and though he enjoyed the time as a warrior, he now was ready to return to his wife and children whom he had not seen for almost four years.

On the voyage to Lamu, Njage looked at the great ocean from the bow of the ship. It put him in a trance making him both nostalgic about all he had seen and been through in his short life.

My early years were filled with peace, joy, and play on the green hills of Kirinyaga (Mt. Kenya). He could envision that great mountain as if he where there this moment! He could see the jagged peak covered in the purest white and encircled by a white cloud with the bright blue sky contrasting with the whiteness. This was his home!

I see my mother preparing food and my younger brothers running around the fire. I am herding the goats with their frolicking kids! I am bathing naked in the cool mountain streams with my age mates.

Immediately, his mind turned, and visions flashed

quickly: dressed as a warrior, raiding for cattle; the astounding vision of Horne on the great horse; the Council of Elders ostracizing him for doing Horne's bidding; marrying his lovely wife, Njuri; seeing his children for the first time; then, suddenly blinded by the reflected light of *Murungu's* (God's) white halo around *Kirima Kia Maara* (Mt. Kenya)!

Oh! How I miss my Njuri and seeing my children.

He then thought about his first trip to Nairobi, the war, the tactics of the Germans, and, in sharp contrast, how Horne had stripped him of his warrior status and manhood. Now, however, he had regained status and honor from the British. He, Njage, now had a rank equal to Horne's. He thought, *maybe this is the way for us Africans to regain our independence, manhood, and pride.*

Again, his bright mind could not rest. *Submit or protest, follow orders or rebel?*

He was awakened from his daydream by some of the Somalis who had been to Lamu before. They explained the place, that it was composed of many islands, some of which were nearly uninhabited. The islands were spread out on far north coast close to Italian Somalia. In that moment, he heard a voice inside him, the voice of his ancestors spoken through the elders:

"Your ancestors began their trek to the mountain. They lived on an island surrounded by the great saltwater. The water parted and they escaped, some in the morning, some in the evening, and some at night. This is why we have different clans. The island was known as Mbwaa!"

Suddenly he knew. *Murungu* and the *Nkoma* were leading him back to the place of his ancestors. The place where the Meru girl was taken to marry, many, many years ago in the time of the great Lawi, the founding father of his clan. He would find her descendants! They were of his people! He slept well and deeply that night as the ship bunk cradled him and swayed gently.

CHAPTER 28

NJAGE ARRIVES IN LAMU
(early 1918)

The dhow entered the large calm harbor between Lamu and Manda islands on a clear sunlit morning. The water sparkled and the white coral houses seemed to grow out of the landscape organically. Many white minarets pierced the dark blue sky. The ship anchored and they boarded a small boat and headed to the landing. It was a busy harbor with all sizes of dhows and boats. They arrived directly in front of the government house facing the inlet.

Njage told the Somalis to wait for him near the harbor wall. Njage entered and saluted the British officer sitting at the main desk.

"And who are you, Boy?"

Njage had not been addressed as "Boy" for a while. He was taken off guard and stuttered.

"Nj-ja-gge, Sir. I have orders from General Smuts," presenting the official documents, his and the Somalis.

"*Karibu!* Welcome! You made it! I had a radio message

from Smuts saying you would be arriving any day. Good. Are all the Somalis well?"

"Sir, most are fine. Some have minor wounds, but they have been attended to. About ten need hospital care."

"Ok. The bursar will pay them. He is in the outer office. Have them sign. I will arrange for hospital for the others. Then I will arrange for their transport to British Somaliland in a few days. Tell them that and oversee the operation. Is that clear?"

"Yes, Sir. *Asante.*"

"Good work, Boy. All seems in order. You seem to be a Boy from upcountry, is that not correct?"

"Yes, Sir. Meru district, Sir."

"It is a long way. Smuts speaks highly of you. I will set your passage to Mombasa, and then a train ticket to Nairobi. Sorry I cannot find you transport all the way to Meru. Check in the office in Nairobi when you arrive."

"Sir, if I may, I would like to stay here a few days. I would like to search for a distant relative."

"Certainly. This is the least we can do. You have served British East Africa well. Come back in a few days, when you are ready to head back."

"Thank you, sir,!"

Njage took the Somalis to the bursar and saw that they and he were paid. The sick were transported to the hospital and the others to the camp outside the town.

Njage left encouraged that he could remain for a few days, but his mind was still ruminating over how he was addressed. Some things had changed for the better, but that "Boy" remark put him in a foul mood.

Once he entered the winding narrow streets and alleys, he entered a different world. He was in a very different far-off place. Men in white robes and women in black *buibui*. Indian men in long shirts, women in colorful saris, and Somali women in their native dress. The few whites he saw were dressed in safari hunting gear.

He came to a large open space near a very large mosque. The *muezzin* had just called the noon prayer, and he could see men through the open windows of the mosque bowing and praying and chanting. It was completely peaceful. He sat on the bench near the mosque and thought, "But how am I to find my relative, the descendent of the daughter of the Lawi?"

As the prayers ended, men and boys were exiting the mosque. One young man came and sat on the concrete bench along the wall where Njage sat.

"*Hujambo* Bwana, I am Hamisi."

"And I Njage."

"You are a stranger, *kweli* (right)?"

"*Kweli*. I have returned from the war and had one more duty here, before heading home - upcountry, to Meru, near *Kirinyaga* (Mt. Kenya)."

"O! How I wish I could travel there! Some of our people go west from here on trading missions in great caravans. There are fewer now since the British arrived. Long ago there were even slave caravans, but once the British took control, the slave trade was outlawed, and many people arrested. But alas, I am just the son of a fisherman."

"Perhaps you can help. I am looking for a family of traders. Many, many years ago a caravan stopped in my country and one of your men married a beautiful Meru girl from my tribe. My ancestors are descended from her brother, who remained in Meru."

"We have many traders, but the oldest family that goes

back to the time when the Persians first arrived might help you. He knows many people. Their leader now is Sharif. Come here tomorrow and I will introduce you. Sharif comes for prayer at this time. He has already left today.

"You are fortunate to be here at this time. It is the Maulidi Feast in a few days. It is our Prophet's birthday. There will be many pilgrims and festivities. All the town's people will gather and sing the names of Allah! There will be sword dancing in this square by the Friday Mosque. Once the fast is broken there will be much good food. Glad you will be here to see this celebration. It is the best time of the year!"

"*Asante sana*, Hamisi. I am very grateful. Thank you for your hospitality. *Tutaonana kesho* (We will see each other tomorrow)!"

"*Karibu* Bwana. *Allah ni mkubwa!* (Welcome. God is great!)"

The next day Hamisi introduced Njage and Sharif. They talked for a great while near the mosque and Sharif invited him for dinner. He lived in a large multistory house a few paces up an alley from the sea. They entered through a large carved door and entered a quiet place so different from the street. There was a pool at the center of the courtyard and many balconies on the upper floors. Men and women scurried here and there on the upper floors. They climbed to the upper story, which was open to the sky. They sat on large pillows around a great carpet with the other male family members, as the women brought dish after dish of sumptuous, delicious dishes — rice colored with turmeric, ginger fish with dates and coconut, meat flavored with cumin, and fruits of every kind. Finally, the women brought a cake made of cashews, honey, and cardamom. Njage never had tasted anything like this.

Sharif noticed Njage enjoying the bounty. He surmised it was the first good meal he had had in a very long while.

"Njage, are you satisfied with this food?"

Njage put a large morsel into his mouth and licking his fingers, replied, "O Bwana, I have never tasted anything like this and the war rations were only posho and sometimes wild game, that is, if we could hunt it ourselves. Our upcountry food is good and filling, but rather bland. We don't use any spice. This is so good and so different."

"*Asante*, I am glad you find this food pleasing. Now to business. You have said that a relative of yours came to Lamu to stay?"

Njage dipped his fingers into the water bowl and began to explain. "Yes, my ancestor, many grandfathers ago, had many children. There were two siblings, a brother and sister. I am descended from the brother. The sister was a very lovely girl. It was very, very long ago, long before the British arrived. Our elders tell of a caravan arriving in our village to trade, and the leader, a young Swahili Arab, seeing this lovely girl, asked for her to be his wife. It was agreed, she left, and was never seen again. I have always wondered about what happened to her. Our tribe honors our ancestors and I would like to know if her spirit rests or if it is wandering without a home. Did she arrive safely? Did she have descendants?"

Sharif's eyes widened and stared in silence, first at the old *mzee* (elder) sitting at the far corner, then at Njage. At last he said, "An interesting tale! And if I tell you we have a similar tale in our family, will it shock you?"

Njage's face was full of surprise. Could this be the connection with Meru? Finally, he said, "Sharif, I find this surprising and almost unbelievable. Do you think our tales are connected? My great grandfather, Sabari, told my father many legends of our tribe's past. Slowly I was let into my tribes lore. I often wondered if these had any truth or proof. He not only told me of the unlikely marriage between this Swahili man and the beautiful Meru girl, but also how our tribe found our home on *Kirinyaga* (Mt. Kenya). How we once lived on an island not far from here called Mbwaa and how we had to leave when we were threatened by sea people. We trekked many years before we reached the Mountain."

Sharif, after having seen the approval on the *mzee's* face, began to speak. "Our family's tale begins with Omari, the son of the founder of our business. He ventured far and traded in all things. His brother Mohammed was involved in the slave trade, so slaves were captured and brought back on the same caravan. But Omari was not like the rest of them. He never approved of slavery.

When he arrived upcountry, so the story goes, he found a lovely maiden whom he married and brought back. Our whole family is descended from Omari and his wife. I think my grandfather knows the tale and even her name.

Mohammed inherited the business from Sharif, the father, but Mohammed also died shortly after of a terrible disease. He was a profligate man whom *Shetani* used to sow hatred among people. Upon his death, Omari inherited the business and refused to deal in slaves. Allah has smiled on us since then and we have all profited. Our stories connect with each other through Omari's marriage."

A voice spoke up in the distance from the old *mzee* (elder) seated on layers of pillows on the other side of the large rooftop:

"O! Allah is great! I know this history well. Omari married Mahiri!"

Njage could not believe his ears! "But Mahiri is a Meru name! We have many women with the name in our clan! Could it be we are distant cousins?"

Other family members helped the mzee, Sharif's grandfather, rise and gave him a cane to steady himself. He slowly approached Njage as he spoke, "Very possible! This is all very possible! There are no other stories like this in Lamu. It is written on our chart. Come with me and I will show you."

Njage was led into another room where a large scroll was in a niche in the wall among many others. It was unwound. Njage could not read, and the writing was very different than what he saw the British use.

Pointing at the chart, the grandfather continued, "We carefully record all our births and deaths in this chart since arriving here long ago from Persia. For example, see here!" Grandfather pointing, "I am *Omari bin Sharif bin Akili,* etc. etc. (Omari, son of Sharif, son of Akili, etc. etc.) And up further, near the top we see *Omari bin Sharif* married to Mahiri whose son was Akili! We, in this family, are all descended from Akili whose mother was Mahiri! So, we too are partly of the Meru tribe!"

Sharif noticed Njage's amazed look and offered, "You must stay with us so we can better know each other before you need to leave."

"Yes, this has been a wonderful evening. I wish I could read your language. Your writing is so much more intricate than that of the British, and more beautiful! So many colors and curlicues!

I will remain a few days more, but I need to return to my wife and children. I have not seen them for almost 4 years."

Sharif, replacing the ancestry roll to its safe nook in the wall, "Let us rest now and we will talk more tomorrow and I will show you around our fine city which has existed for hundreds of years.

We will also visit some of the other islands where there are settlements from thousands of years ago. One of these islands is called Manda. It has many old ruins. Perhaps it is the same isle your tribe called Mbwaa. It has strange tides which sometimes allow passage to the mainland. Your legends may not be so far-fetched at all. Our old ancestors were wise and knew how to preserve our histories even before writing.

"Feel at home now. You may stay here with us until you have to leave. This in fact is the same house that welcomed Mahiri so long ago. It is also yours. We are so happy you have come."

And so, the bond was formed and Njage felt gratified to have found the answer to the riddle that plagued him since the first time he was told the old legends. He was grateful to Sabari, Muthamia, Kithingi and all the other Meru Elders for preserving the tribe's history. His tribe had trekked from this place, he had returned as had Mahiri and he would take this knowledge back to Meru. It was completing the great circle of life.

Njage had now become even more proud of his Meru roots, his elders' wisdom, and his culture. As he pondered all he had seen and heard, he thought, *how much had been preserved! How much more difficult to remember the past without the benefit of writing! How talented were his ancestors! Though they lacked the tools of the British, or even the Swahili, they have survived and prospered and remembered!*

He now realized that he and his friends had the ability to take back the control of their lives. Soon, they would be free again! Soon, powerful and free! Soon, Soon!

CHAPTER 29

LAIKISAT GOES TO WAR (1914-15)

Laikisat and some fellow *Il-murran* had been accepted by Lord Delamare to patrol the border with German Tanganyika. They left in a great caravan passing through Hell's gate near Mount Longonot and travelled miles through the dry Rift Valley to the west side of Kilimanjaro. There was little food and great thirst, but they persevered. Colonists had formed vigilantes to try to secure the border. The rangers were few — some of Berkley Cole's Somali Scouts on horseback, and some of Wessle's and Booker's scouts.[16] Most of the white colonials and British and South African regulars formed the major contingent headed to Taveta on the other side of Kilimanjaro, where the *Wajerumani* (Germans) had crossed the border and taken the town.

Arriving at the border, the Maasai were strung along in groups at the points where they could report and defend incursions. At this point at the border the Rift Valley narrows to only 84 km., as it is hemmed in by the Mau escarpment and the foothills of Kilimanjaro. As Laikisat and his group camped one night, they heard a distant roar. An incessant drumming on the ground which at first was like a low-pitched hum, but, hour by hour, grew closer and louder.

As light dawned, Laikisat jumped up. *"Ona, Ona!* Look at the dust on the horizon. Now, see, see, many beasts!"

As they stared, they saw thousands of wildebeests heading south. "This is what the elders spoke of - the great migration!"

One of his fellow murran exclaimed, "I have never seen so many! Will they trample us? Prepare yourselves!"

Neither had Laikisat ever seen such a sight! Wildebeest, zebra, and all manner of animals, stretching from horizon to horizon, stampeding. He just stared, as the others urged him:

"Laikisat, run, run!"

They all began running to a small hillock about one-hundred meters in the distance. Laikisat was the last to make it up the hill, before they were surrounded by the stampeding animals. As they stared, they could see zebra, antelope, and the occasional lion, giraffe, rhino and elephant intermingled in the seemingly unending sea of animals!

"Ngai anakuja! God is coming! So many, so many!" yelled Laikisat.

An excited murran responded, "Let us try to spear some for meat. When we spy an antelope close to the bottom of the hill, that is moving more slowly, let us throw our spears!"

"Yes, we will have a good feed tonight!"

After downing a few antelope, they sat and waited until

the rampage passed and headed toward the river. Now they could see the wildebeests plunging down the steep banks of the Maara River, followed by zebra, elephant, lion, and every other conceivable animal. It was spectacular! Some of the bank fell away under the weight of the multitude, some of the animals were drowned, others plunged and used the bodies of others as bridges. Only the strong crossed safely.

This continued until dusk, until most had crossed or drowned. The din faded into the night. The weak perished so that the strong could survive. Laikisat remembered this lesson. He added it to his memory. It was very useful knowledge gained from this spectacular event!

In the meantime, some of the murran had climbed down and were dragging up a wildebeest and two gazelle that were slain. They were happy to be able to eat well that evening. The evening was peaceful, and they ate heartily.

But with the setting of the sun, they noticed storm clouds gathering and heard thunder in the distance. Soon huge drops of rain were pounding all around them.

They had seen an outcropping of rock earlier near the bottom of the hill protected from the rain. They ran carrying some of their meat and were able to find shelter. The outcropping led to a small cave where they found warmth and protection from the storm.

The rains now had intensified to a fury! They filled their calabashes with the fresh rainwater and drank heartily before falling into a deep sleep. They were lulled to sleep by the soothing sound of the rain and their full bellies. That night, *Ngai* had smiled on them!

At first light, that wonderful African dawn after a rain, when the sky is deep blue and the light infuses every corner of the world, Laikisat looked out on *Ngai's* creation and gave thanks for all that he had seen and that Ngai had kept them all safe one more day. He knew this would only last for a breath, because once the sun rises, the heat returns with a vengeance, and new problems and adventures would arise with the sun.

Now with the dust settled in the clear air, he was able to see the Germans' encampment clearly, but the white tents were shredded! Nothing remained but tatters of cloth.

The others awoke and they slowly and carefully made their way south. They found a narrow point in the river where logs had fallen across and made a temporary bridge. There was utter destruction at the camp! Body parts and crushed utensils were strewn everywhere. Because the wind was from the south and because they must have eaten and drunk well, the Germans had been oblivious to the stampede. There were piles of bones. The lions must have also had a fine supper! Some of the tents were carried off by the rushing waters. The torrential rains had caused a flash flood, which filled the entire valley. Laikisat and his fellow murran resolved to march back to the ranger station to report what they had witnessed.

Laikisat just stared and took this all in. Truly *Ngai* was great!

CHAPTER 30

LORD DELAMARE, WEEKS, AND MAASAI ANGER (1917-18)

From his first travels to East Africa Lord Delamare had Somali and Maasai companions and friends. Though he was a firm proponent of the white settlers and stood up for their rights and did much for agriculture, nevertheless he was also a firm supporter of the Maasai.

As early as 1915 the Native Followers Recruitment Ordinance enabled the military to conscript Africans for war duties. The Council put this law into effect in early 1916. The need for recruits steadily increased. Though many willingly served, many Africans avoided assisting the authorities. The Maasai outwardly refused. By 1918 the government pressed for the Maasai to be conscripted. Delamare objected because he held that theirs was a great service in providing beef and mutton for hungry troops and a hungry nation.

Governor Bowring ordered Mr. Weeks to arrange a conference to put the conscription law into force. The

Maasai had always refused to carry *Kitambulisho* (ID's) and now, also, to register for conscription. The government had finally put Mr. Weeks in charge to execute the conscription.

The *murran* near Narok had paid no attention to the order to register and had scattered into the forest and far plains. Weeks, who spoke no Maasai or any African language, had the KAR try to find the ringleaders. They heard the *murran* were near a small village. Though they found the village almost deserted, some askaris fired and killed two old women and injured a number of other innocents.

When Delamare heard this, he was incensed and wired a protest to the Governor. In the meantime, the *murran* became infuriated. They roamed the plains in anger, burning and creating havoc on the nearby farms and in the towns. A full rebellion was developing. Several East Indians were killed, and much damage was done.

Delamare left at once with some of his trusted *murran* along with a Maasai, Mesobero, his head herder. Among these were Laikisat and Koinet. Mesobero explained they had come in peace. Delamare carried on a long discussion in Maasai with the rebellious warriors.

Then Mesobero discovered one of his own brothers was killed by the KAR. Discussions collapsed and Delamare returned to Narok with his *murran*. Later they all again returned to restart negotiations. A compromise settlement was negotiated.

In this episode Delamare discovered that Mesobero was a man of honor. Though still aggrieved over the loss of his brother, he remained loyal to Delamare.

This affected Laikisat profoundly. On his way home back to the camp, he had a great deal of time to put all this in perspective.

Both Lordi D and Mesobero are true fine men and murran, thought Laikisat. *I respect their bravery and honesty. They are tough men. They can be severe. But their qualities of empathy and forgiveness are never forgotten. We Maasai also try to practice these characteristics. We sometimes fail, as all men do, but it is important to try. I will dedicate myself to the code of the murran in whatever Ngai puts in my path!*

The Maasai never were conscripted. The war soon ended and there was no longer a need. Only those like Laikisat and Koinet helped with the actual war effort since they were friends of Delamare and volunteered to help him.

The Maasai remain an independent and proud tribe to this day. Members of other tribes who did not wish to be conscripted often went to live with the Maasai. Kamau wa Ngeni was one of many such Gikuyu, and he would soon play a major role in the history of East Africa.[17]

CHAPTER 31

THE END IN SIGHT (1918)

These last few weeks found the capital in disarray. By 1918 most of the fighting had moved far west and south. First soldiers were returning dead and wounded from the battles. They were white, brown, and black. The *Kariakor* had suffered many casualties from the long treks with lack of food. The Kings African Rifles and British and South African troops fared the same. No sooner had they arrived, than the plague of influenza struck. The lack of rain and poor agricultural output and the monetary crisis were hitting everyone. The Colony's very survival was at stake.

Men were being released from service to go back to their farms and families. Gichuru was stamping *Vitambulisho* (Id's) with release stamps for all types of service in the war effort.

Of the over one million African porters in East Africa, ninety thousand porters had perished. This included over forty-five thousand fatalities among the King's *Kariakor*. Over one-hundred-twenty-seven thousand troops of all nationalities participated in the actual fighting in East

Africa. Some had even been to north Africa, Europe, and India to fight for the Empire. This had decimated entire villages of men.[18]

Njage with his slight limp approached Gichuru's office. He thought about the long treks in the heat and the dying men of the *Kariakor* and wondered if the Kamba man ever returned to Machakos to his wife and children. Njage considered himself watched over by the *Nkoma*, the good spirits of his ancestors.

He had recovered well from both the wound and the influenza, though it still was raging, and many people were sick and dying. He had seen so many on the coast, and even here as he entered the capital. His mind was full of the memories of the suffering of all men, both of the Europeans, as well as of his fellow Africans. So many injured men cried for help in their time of fear, pain, and panic. After the suffering in the war, the pandemic carried so many more away into the next world.

The suffering was shared equally by all. *Murungu* (God) and the *Nkoma* (Spirits) heard the cries of some but ignored many others. Njage heard men imploring the names of many gods. *Murungu* seemed indifferent to the god-name they used or their tribe. None was spared solely because of race, or goodness, or tribe.

Gichuru saw Njage through his office window and his face lit up as he saw his friend approach. He had lost track of his many friends who left to take part in the war. He had repressed his fears of their safety, which now were resurfacing with the troops returning. His own brother was involved in the long attack on Tanga, and news had arrived in the early days of the war of his death and burial near Salaita. He could not dwell on these losses. There were

so many of his friends and acquaintances who returned
maimed or did not return at all.

But now he was overjoyed to see his good friend Njage
approaching. He now ran out to greet Njage!

"*Rafiki, rafiki! Habari?* How are you? So glad you have
returned."

"*Hujambo!* Gichuru! *Mungu Alinisaidia!* God helped me!
I am very fine. See. In one piece and going home soon!"

"Njage! You are injured!"

"O, just a slight wound, but healing. The fever was worse,
but that too was washed away in the short rains. Many
died from the influenza. I was fortunate. I was fortunate
to have good assistance each time. At Salaita there was a
fine mission doctor who attended to my leg. The same was
true during my fever. The white sisters in those very large
hats were so good to me. They nursed me back to health
when so many died. There are some very good and selfless
Wazungu (Europeans)!"

"Come. I'll stamp your *Kitambulisho* (ID) and then please
come and stay a few days at the *shamba*."

"Thank you. I do need a rest before the long trip home.
I have been traveling for over six months, from Dar es
Salaam to Lamu and Mombasa. I have seen so much of
this great East Africa! So many treasures and fine people
of all tribes. I had never imagined the greatness and the
beauty of the land and the people. I will tell you about it.
It has made me think much of our past and future. If only
we could unite and rule ourselves. I have seen all kinds of
men across our land. So many brave and intelligent people
in every tribe I encountered. I am sure we are destined to
be a great nation someday!"

"Shhh. Do not speak so loudly. You are used to being in

the bush. Here the very trees have ears! There are stirrings here especially among the East Indians. The government is not happy. We can talk later at home.

I received word from a Maasai who was here yesterday that Laikisat will be here tomorrow. Lord Delamare's Maasai are passing through Nairobi on their way home. They will parade on Victoria Street and Government Road!"

"It will be so good to see Laikisat and catch up on his adventures - or what we thought would be simply excitement and adventure. Now I see what war is like. What devastation it has caused! It is an ugly devil. *Shetani* has visited us!"

The next day they watched the parade led by the Lord sitting on his great horse marching in front of his Maasai. His remarks were full of good and thankful words for their defending the border with German East Africa, which now had become a British protectorate. He told them in Maasai that they had served the Crown very well.

When the formalities were over, Gichuru approached Laikisat.

"*Suba,* Laikisat! After your dismissal come to my shamba tonight and we will catch up on our news. We three have much to talk about."

"*Suba!* I am so glad to see both of you, *marafiki* (friends)! So good to see that both of you have survived your trials. We can now become reacquainted. We will not sleep tonight. There is much to tell."

"Yes tonight. *Kwaheri.*"

BOOK 6:

NO WAR. NO PEACE

CHAPTER 32

THE WITCHMEN
(Very Early 1918)

One evening after supper, Gichuru retired to his hut for a rest after a very long day of dealing with the returning veterans, wives and others who were looking for family members, paying their *Kipande* (Tax), or issuing *Kitambulisho* (ID's) to those males just reaching age fifteen. Most Gikuyu had become resigned to following colonial directives.

Arriving home late, he went directly to his hut and fell into a deep sleep.

Sometime after midnight he awoke startled. Drums were beating in the distance. He thought he heard some sounds and commotion outside. He rose, grabbed his *panga* (machete), but as he exited, he was jumped from behind, muzzled, and carried up the hills into the forest behind his *shamba*.

After quite a long, blindfolded walk, he was untied deep within the forest. He was ordered to sit by a large fire around which he saw many Witchmen dancing and singing oathing songs and calling upon the spirits of their ancestors. At once he realized that this was one of the illegal gatherings which Njage had told him about. In Meru country it was called a *Kiama*. Gichuru knew from his work with Horne that such meetings were banned long ago in Gikuyu land, but he also knew that they were still held in secret. He had never participated or even knew when or where they were held. He wondered why he had been brought here.

Finally, the most ancient of the participants began speaking in a loud voice: "We are here for we are tired! Tired of our shackles. Tired of losing land, paying *Kipande* (Tax)! We want release from carrying tags around our necks like dogs and following rules which are not ours. Our people in the Reserve want assistance. All these trials of war, plague, and famine have made them want answers. They want a better life. Our people need to be organized. We can help, but we need leaders. Men who will lead and unite our people. Men who can speak to the Wazungu (Europeans)!

"You are like a key. You can open doors for us to freedom! You sit with many white men, you know the men on the Council, even the Governor!

"Gichuru, we have brought you here because you are powerful, one of the few Africans who has risen among the whites. Now that the war is almost over, we need you. Even after the perils of war, the evil *Nkoma* (Spirits) have sent plague and famine. Our people cannot breathe, there is much fluid in their chest. They have high fever. Many have already died. Now the rains are late!

"Swear now that you will assist us!

"For now, we do not want violence, we need you to

use your powers of speech. We will wait until we see the fruits of your labors. We have seen how the East Indians are moving into the Council, but we, the rightful owners of this land, have no place. Instead they wish to place a white holy man to represent us, as if we have no mind, speech, or hearing. He is well meaning, but he is not us! They dishonor our ancestors. There are others among us of importance who have already sworn. Some have formed groups like the Indians. You will meet them if you swear loyalty!

"Swear now! Swear! Swear and drink the cup of blood. Do you swear?"

Gichuru tried to gather words as his head pounded and he felt his eyes bulging from his face. "Wait! *Mzee* (Old Man), wait! First, know that what I do and have done is for my family and my people. I have tried to keep the elders informed and not be a traitor to our people. If I did not do this work, they would find others, even from other tribes to carry out their work."

The elder Witchman placed his face close to Gichuru. "We know that you are a good man, a loyal Gikuyu man. That is why we have brought you here. We also know you have friends among the Kamba, Meru, and Maasai. This will be helpful to us.

"Swear now before we tell you more! Drink and swear!"

At this the drums grew louder still. The other Witchmen danced around the fire. Some were taken by the Nkoma (Spirits) and convulsed on the ground speaking with the voice of the ancestors: "We are in agony because of the suffering of our people! Free them and us! Relieve us! Give us fresh breath!"

A second Witchman came close to Gichuru with a cup

and a torch and held it close to his face and peered deeply into his eyes: *"Aikaragia mbia ta njuu ngigi!* (He is a man who looks after many, as the njuu bird looks after the locusts!) They are saving us to consume us, first slowly, then our children!"

This was an old proverb that Gichuru knew well. The Witchman was comparing the Governor and the Council to ravenous birds.

"Drink now! Swear to your people or you will face the consequences!" Continued the Witchman.

Gichuru gulped hard as he said with his voice quavering, "I have always been faithful to my people, to this land which provides us with so much! I do swear to be loyal to our people, to the Gikuyu first, but to all Africans until we are free. I swear upon my ancestors that you may trust me! I will serve only my Gikuyu brothers!"

With this they passed the cup and Gichuru drank deeply. He was moved and shaken by what he had seen. Obviously, events were moving rapidly, and he no longer had control. He had accepted for his children, so that they might be free.

The men quickly disappeared into the dark night. Only Gichuru and the elder remained by the fire. They talked until dawn. What the elder was sharing and asking was making him feel his life was about to enter a much more dangerous phase.

But the longer they talked, the more Gichuru's heart lightened. His fear gradually left him. *Ngai* (God) and the good *Nkoma* (Spirits) had taken him this far and he would trust that this decision was the right one. He would face the rocks and pits of the road with bravery. There was no other way. The plan and the path were opening before him.

CHAPTER 33

NJAGE RETURNS TO MERU
(late 1918)

Njage's trip home to Meru usually followed the western trek around Mt. Kenya. It was difficult going up and down the steep ravines. However, since the arrival of the *Wazungu* (Europeans) and the many settler farms on the western side of the mountain, there were improved dirt roads and more carts and horseless carriages on the east side of the mountain. He decided it might take less time and he would be able to get rides on trucks or other vehicles.

His time with Gichuru and Laikisat had renewed their friendship and they all had agreed that after they reconnected with their families and tribes, they would meet again. They all realized that they needed to act because these years had taken a bad toll on their people." Njage was still not sure where this would lead, but he knew Gichuru's placement in the capital would inform them. Laikisat's relation to Lord Delamare also would help them crystallize their plans.

As he began his trek, his eyes were really opened by the large amounts of land under cultivation. Huge tracts owned by colonials were filled with maize, wheat, and cattle. The higher up the mountain, the more land was in colonial hands. He saw coffee and then tea. The colonials in Nairobi now even referred to this area as the White Highlands.

There were many European style homes on the hills with small huts for the African workers and servants. Again, he felt conflicted. This land had been mostly vacant before the coming of the *Wazungu*. Though there were no villages, the land was used by his people and others for grazing. But why should the colonists have the right to it? Yes, they are producing food, coffee, and tea, but most of this was for their benefit and export, not his people.

Gichuru had told Njage that more colonials would be arriving soon. The British were offering the British veterans cheap land to farm in these Highlands. The colonials employed many Africans to do the back-breaking farm work. They paid them but a pittance and most lived separate from their families. They were mostly men whose wives and relatives remained in the Reserve working on their small *shambas* (farms). They worked the land with only *pangas* (machetes) and had none of the machines that the *Wazungu* employed. This left the men lonely to look for escape with drink and womanizing.

Upon arriving at his home in Meru, Njage went down the road to his family's *shamba*. It was not far from where Horne had built his log cabin. Horne was nowhere to be seen. He stopped short to notice a large wooden building where his huts once stood. His huts, grain storage, and plantings were all gone! All was replaced by a *Wazungu* (European) compound!

He stood frozen! He was angry, sad, and desperate!

Then he noticed a person coming up the hill. It was a distant relative whom he recognized, "*Muga*, Kiria! (Greetings, Kiria)"

"Njage, is that you? You have returned, *rafiki* (friend)! I am so happy to see you after all this time. We did not know how you fared in the War. There has been no news. Thank *Murungu* (God) that it is over. Your wife was very worried."

"But what has happened to my Njuri, my house, my livelihood? I am in shock! Is she well? Are the *Nkoma* (Spirits) playing with me!"

"T-t-t-t! Njage! You must not have heard. Horne has left and we have a new District Officer. The Methodist mission needed more land to build their school. They confiscated your *shamba* (fields). Your Njuri was given land further east and south in the Reserve. I will show you. There was much commotion here."

"But are they well? Murungi, my son! Kithingi, my father! The others! I should never have left! I thought *Murungu* and Horne would keep them safe since I was helping the British! I should not have trusted *Kangangi* (Horne)! Now I find that my loyalty was misplaced. I should have never accepted being chief or going to fight. None of them are to be trusted!"

"O *Ndugu yangu*! My brother do not blame yourself. We all do what we think is best to survive. We all have bowed to these foreigners, but our day will come."

"So how are my parents? Family?"

"Njuri is fine, though it was hard to rebuild the huts and put the new land into cultivation. Your children are growing strong and they are a big help. Let us go. Njuri will tell you more. Better she tells you herself. She will be overjoyed to finally see you again."

So off they trekked about ten kilometers to the small village of Nkubu. It was a very lovely part of Meru with vistas to the plains below and Mount Ithinguni and Mt. Kenya above. His new land was close to a clear mountain river, the Thingithu.

Njage had been through this place when the Catholics had received land in Mujwa for their new mission further down the mountain. He was pleased with this location because it was some distance from the District Office in Meru, but as he approached the village, he worried about what he would find.

"*Muga*, Njuri! I am back!"

Njuri dropped her *mchi* (pestle) which she was using to grind the maize and with astonishment yelled out, "*Mugamano, mugamano*! O *Murungu* (God) is good! Finally, you are back! I thought I would never see you again, husband. All my troubles are nothing now that you are returned."

"O, how I missed you. So long a separation, but now I am here to help with all our misfortunes."

"It has been quite an awful few years! But finally, we just now have a crop in spite of the lack of rain. The Thingithu River has provided us with clean water and good irrigation. The children help with carrying water. It has been hard, but not as hard on us as on your father and your brother.

When the new D.O. told us we had to move, your brother was angered. His temper flared! I had never seen him so angry. He refused for us to move as did your father. In his youthful anger, Ikiara took his *rungu* (wooden mace) and struck one of the guards. The D.O. witnessed all of it! The guard fell almost dead! But the protective *Nkoma* (Spirits) were good. The guard survived, but they carried Ikiara to the jail and beat him mercilessly.

"Your father also refused to leave. He just sat on the ground until they carried him away also to jail. He refused to eat in that dark place and became deaf and mute. He was passing quickly into the world of the *Nkoma*. When the D.O. saw that father was leaving this world, he recanted and let them both your father and brother go. We have nursed them both back, but they are very bitter, like the leaves of the *miraa*![19]"

"Njuri, I am so sorry. I am here to help now. I am ashamed. I could not protect you and our family, while I fought for these British *Wazungu* in whom I placed my trust. I had misgivings about placing my hope in them, but I was so distraught about being a go-between. I needed a change. Now I realize my loyalty was misplaced. I should have never left. I should have returned sooner!"

"This is not your doing. You thought you were protecting us. You could not have left your command. How could you have known that another DO was coming. Come now, you must be tired. You have not seen your grown children. Your daughter is cooking. We will eat and revive our family life.

"But I see you limping! You have been injured! But at least you are returned."

"You are so good to me. I am so happy to be back. But, no, I am fine. Just a slight wound and recovering from the plague. I am strong and well.

"But now that I see all that has befallen us, I am even more determined to change things."

"Let us go and see the others." With this Njage rested and settled down to a quiet life. He cultivated his crops and stayed away from Meru and the D.O. His life as a go-between was over. He wanted nothing to do with them. But in his mind, he knew he soon would be back in Nairobi with Gichuru and Laikisat.

How did he know?

My ancestors are telling me what I must now do. It was a clarity of mind. *What had happened and is happening here and what I have seen on my long journeys have crystallized into ideas. Some dangerous ideas. But if successful might change my life, that of my people, and history. I must soon meet with my two marafiki (friends) who have become like brothers.*

CHAPTER 34

NAIROBI (1918-1923)

T he end of the WWI brought celebration to Nairobi and East Africa, even though 1918-19 were hard years because of the influenza pandemic which gripped East Africa and the rest of the world, and because of the prolonged drought which followed. British East Africa was also experiencing growing and financial pains after the war. There were economic difficulties in the colony due to huge deficits and the limited trade.

This continued after 1920 when the East African Protectorate became a British Crown Colony. Gichuru saw how many men - European, Indian, and African - had been injured and were now returning. Many more had not returned. He saw how many Europeans soldiers, both those who had fought in East Africa and elsewhere for the Empire, were offered good terms to settle in Kenya. He saw how the lands north of Nairobi between Gikuyu lands and Meru lands were now called the White Highlands. Lands which had always been African, even though uninhabited, were being claimed by these interlopers. All this added to the turmoil of Gichuru and the Non-Europeans. In spite of all this most people tried to settle into a more normal life.

There were also disagreements between settlers and Indian immigrants. Many Indians had been living in the coastal cities as a result of trade with British India. They had lived there for centuries. At the time of the building of the railroad, other Indian coolies were brought over from the British Indian Empire to help with its construction. Many others moved inland to establish *dukas* (small shops). White settlers felt outnumbered and pressed Downing Street and Parliament to limit Asian immigration.

Njage had noticed how populated the western slopes of Kirimara (Mt. Kenya) were with *Wazungu* (Europeans). Now ex-British soldier settlers were also being given land grants here. This added to stirring the pot of dissatisfaction.

Most church men also sided with the settlers because they feared the overwhelming of their western Christian values under the pressure of animist, Moslem, and East Indian belief systems. Only a few missionaries thought the Africans should have a voice in their government. Ever so many of these missionaries wanted a more gradual extension of the African voice. They believed a more educated African populace was needed before giving them an equal voice. Africans were the only group that the British thought needed to prove themselves before being granted representation.

The government was going through all sorts of meetings and disagreements both in East Africa and London, trying to adjust to the economic difficulties as well as the question of representation on the Governing Council for East Africa. The new Legislative Council was to have elected representatives among the settlers, but opposition had arisen because the Indian citizens were protesting, also wanting a voice. Should they be represented? How many?

The Indians already outnumbered the Europeans in the general population, but the European settlers were unwilling to give them a voice equal to their numbers. Gichuru knew that the League of Nations had entrusted the British with responsibility to protect the rights of the tribal peoples under the title "Protectorate." He wondered how the voice of the Africans would be resolved. He was not optimistic.

Since near the end of the war, Africans were left entirely out of the discussion. In 1917 it was proposed that there would be elections to the council in 1919. Who would be voting? How would delegates be chosen?

Both the Indian Association of Nairobi, a group representing organized Indians, and the Government of British India were incensed at the unavailability of a voice. They were petitioning and protesting for the vote for Indian inhabitants in East Africa and for not limiting Indian immigration to Africa. This skewed view between Indians and colonials continued to be a problem.

In 1921 there were 9651 Europeans versus 22,822 Indians.[20] The settlers totally ignored the over 2,000,000 African Kenyans. Gichuru felt highly insulted by what many *Wazungu* (Europeans) were saying about the Africans. Gichuru's mind kept rehashing the question: *why should Africans only be allowed representation after they had become educated and westernized? Many Wazungu were less educated than Africans who had been to mission schools!*

As the settlers dug in their heals, they were indifferent to the outrage that was building among the indigenous people. The ingredients for unrest were being spread throughout British East Africa.

More coals were heaped on the fire when, under the leadership of Jeevanjee[21], prominent Indian business and community leaders were unionizing, organizing protests, and petitioning the Legislative Council for a more dominant voice. The Council, the Governor, and Downing Street were trying to resolve the representational problem for years. They were deadlocked.

Gichuru was also aware that Jeevanjee went as far as advocating that East Africa should be added to the British Indian Empire. This pitted them squarely in the face of Lord Delamare, who wanted solely colonial European rule, but with room for shared African representation once they were educated. All this weighed on Gichuru's mind.

Also, at this time Harry Thuku[22], one of the few educated Africans had formed the Young Gikuyu Association. They passed resolutions supporting the Indian positions. However, he was removed after the Gikuyu elders agreed that supporting the Indians was not to their benefit. Gichuru became very upset when Thuku was eventually deported to Somalia for other reasons by the British to prevent him taking part in any further organizing.

The arguments lasted well into 1923 with hardly any satisfaction by any parties involved. Indians were not happy with resolutions to limit Asian immigration. European colonists wanted control. Least happy were Africans, who had only a few sympathetic white missionaries advocating African claims for representation. The fire was heating up and the pot continued to simmer and roll!

Gichuru thought much about these problems while he sipped his tea overlooking the city. *What about we Africans who far outnumber all other inhabitants? The British have always had the demeaning view considering us like children who needed to be slowly incorporated only after education and acculturation. I remember how angry Njage became when he was referred to as Boy. It was so very degrading for him, especially after he had served the British so admirably in the campaigns. We need to demand representation in our own country!*

The arguments on who was to be on the Legislative Council continued for years. The European settlers and the Indians sent delegations to argue their cases to Downing Street. It took until 1923 for a White Paper[23] to be issued by London, which outlined the set-up of the Council and how members would be elected from the different constituencies.

Moreover, there had been a Vigilance Committee formed by European settlers to ensure that their views would hold sway. London proposed that there would be five seats held by Indians, eleven by Europeans, and one Arab. It also stated that Kenya Colonial Government held a trust on behalf of the Africans. The Africans were to be represented by one sympathetic European missionary! Segregation and immigration were to be decided by the Council. This was totally unacceptable to both the Asians and the Africans, including Gichuru!

Though all seemed decided, the test law on immigration never took effect because of a change in the ruling party in London - a Labor government came to power, which was unsympathetic to the European colonists. So still all was unresolved.

Gichuru had gained more and more responsibility in his government job after the war. He felt important. He had many friends among the inhabitants: African, colonists, and Indians. But something was still missing. The war had shown him the vulnerability of all peoples and tribes and their systems of control. Each had their advantages and disadvantages. Gichuru was aware of the debates, discussion, and problems the government was experiencing. He heard and overheard colonists, Indians, and Africans discussing the problems. Change was coming, one way or the other. He decided he must be part of it.

The experience with the Witchmen in the forest had also affected him deeply and he came to see his position and the Africans' plight differently. As 1920 began, his worldview had expanded. He was now concerned about all of his people, not only his immediate family. He saw that he had a responsibility to change the plight of his countrymen.

A few months after his oath taking in the forest, he had come in contact with Grace Wahu[24], a younger woman who had gone to his same mission school in Kabete. She had come in to pay for her family's *Kipande* (Tax). She told him her husband, Kamau Wa Ngengi, had also been educated in a Scottish mission school and that he was getting involved in the East African Union, the EAU. The EAU was unionizing Africans, like the Indians had done with the Indian settlers. They would fight for higher wages and representation on the council. It was based on the Young Kikuyu Association, after Thuku left. Gichuru was very interested and Wahu gave him the details of the meetings.

"Wahu, I have worked in this office during the entire war, collecting *Kipande* and registering the men for conscription."

She looked up and wondered how much she should tell him about her husband, Kamau. After thinking she began,

"I have heard about you from the elders and I believe it is safe to tell you about Kamau. During the war he went to live with his aunt who had married an important Maasai. As you are aware, the Maasai refused conscription, so he remained among that tribe until recently."

Gichuru was not surprised because he knew of many others who had also done so. Shaking his head in agreement, "Yes, we do what we must to survive. I have a very good Maasai friend who had fought to protect the border as one of Lord Delamare's warriors. He also saw the effects of Weeks Raid on the Maasai and the killing of innocents. I hope Kamau can meet Laikisat and also my Meru friend, Njage. I think we will all have much in common with Kamau."

"While Kamau lived with his uncle he took the Maasai name, *Kinyata*[25], meaning *beaded belt* in the Maa language. I will relay what we have talked about to Kinyata. Await my message. I will send word to you about when and where to meet very soon. Kinyata will be happy to hear this news. The Witchmen had told Kinyata that they would send some important men to see him. *Kwaheri* for now."

"*Kwaheri*, Wahu! Good to have met you."

With this Gichuru stared at the growing capital outside his window. Here was his opportunity and that of his friends. He had seen so many changes and now, finally, he saw what he had been prepared to do by his ancestors.

CHAPTER 35

AFRICAN WISDOM AND EXPERIENCE (1921-1923)

Gichuru's hard work during the war years was paying off economically. Though he was happy, and he had a growing family, he was determined to make something more of himself. Though he and his father's family were wealthy by African standards, he wanted to be a *bwana mkubwa* (Important Man) like some of the Europeans, who were building large houses and had expansive plantations.

While still in his teens Gichuru was taken by Kahara, his father, to visit an uncle that lived in Molo. It was an exciting trip, his first time on the Iron Rhino. On the way across the Rift Valley, they passed a magnificent house, almost a castle, where many beautiful horseless carriages were parked. The vehicles had just arrived from the coast on the Iron Rhino and could travel even on the dirt and mud roads. Around the house were many fenced-in acres filled with cattle and sheep. Gichuru was impressed and thought, *why can't I have a house like that some day?* Now, the war had brought more building and more European settlers! Why should he and his clan not be entitled to this same wealth?

He thought about his own Gikuyu tradition: *Ngai (God) had spoken to us from Kirinyaga (Mt. Kenya) and given our tribe all the land around it. Laikisat and the Maasai have a similar tradition about cattle. Ngai had told them they could claim all the cattle. He had said nothing to or about Wazungu (Europeans)!*

The Legislative Council, which had had appointed members, was now to consist of elected representatives. This Council was to work with the Governor to rule the entire country.

I am upset that there is no representation for any Africans, even my own Gikuyu, who have assisted the Wazungu since my father's generation! Thought Gichuru. *I feel confusion, outrage! Kahara has given so much loyalty and service from the time the British first arrived and signed the Gikuyu treaty. He had assisted with translation for many of the Commissioners and Governors. Though now my father is advanced in age, he is still an important elder in the tribe. He too feels unappreciated and unequal. I must act on the oath I have taken in the forest. I must act!*

However, all this just added to the conflict in Gichuru's mind. He still liked many of Europeans with whom he worked, but could not understand why Africans could only go so far. There still was segregation. Africans and Indians were not allowed to settle in certain areas like the White Highlands. Each different tribe had its own Reserve. Gichuru's mind kept ruminating on the same question: *What is the best way to bring about change? Maybe the key was wealth? Maybe once I became rich? I had thought this was the way to attain their respect. Now, I have second thoughts.*

Gichuru learned at the mission that all men were supposedly created equal. It was written in both the white man's Bible and, also, in the Constitution of the United States. He had seen the savagery with which white tribes fought and killed each other. In African tradition, tribes had very strict rules about killing and raiding, about not killing women and children. Whites, even though they had Commandments and prayed often, seemed to have no restrictions when it came to war.

Near the end of the war he had seen tanks, which the Africans in the bush thought of as giant mechanical elephants, shoot fireballs at the enemy. They were also terrified by the airplanes that were like flying mechanical birds dropping fire. These poor people did not know where to run or hide.

Mostly, Gichuru, learned that Europeans were divided among themselves. He saw them dying and miserable. He remembered the stories his father and other *wazee* (old men) recounted near the burning fires. How his people had migrated from the west and had to claim land and fight for its control. He remembered their wisdom: *When your enemies fight each other then is the time to strike. Now is the time to take their cows and their land, which Ngai gave to your forefathers. When the fire begins to burn, throw in more charcoal, lest you have to start it again!*

Kahara, Njage's father, was a wise man. Though now aged and in ill health, Kahara could foresee that European rule would end. It was only a matter of time. He did not know how many moons it would take, but in his mind's eye he could see that the Europeans days were numbered. The unrest was building. He already had seen his son become a great chief respected by them and saw Gichuru achieve his own wealth. His mind had the vision of his grandchildren and great grandchildren living in a free land.

Gichuru, was of the same mind as Kahara. He knew that Europeans were impatient and that to Africans time and patience were their strength. African time was not the white man's time. Maybe, his son would someday rise to be greater than the Great White King in Britain. The Indians he knew had told him that British India was having uprisings because they wanted freedom. Gichuru held this in his mind and heart and asked *Ngai* (God) and the *Nkoma* (Spirits) to show him what his next step should be. He was anxiously awaiting word from Wahu.

CHAPTER 36

The African Dawn (1922)

K amau, or Kinyata, as he was now known, sent Wahu to see Gichuru. Arrangements were made to meet Gichuru and his friends in an isolated area northwest of Kikuyu in the forest above a town known as *Olikijabe*, a Maasai name, meaning *place of the wind.* The Gikuyu felt that good spirits talked to them in this place through the wind.

Early one December morning, Gichuru, Laikisat, and Njage boarded the Iron Rhino at Nairobi Station and headed for the stop at Kijabe. They travelled in the dark. They could only feel the train continuously rising as they approached the highest point near Limuru. They could also hear the steam engine chugging away as it climbed. Even though an extra engine had been added, it took quite a long time to climb the steep winding slopes to the top of the escarpment.

Gichuru had travelled this way once before when he was a teenager. Shortly after the railroad had been completed, Kahara, his father, had decided to take Gichuru to visit his uncle in Molo. The most exciting part was the approach to the escarpment of the Great Rift Valley. What impressed them both was the almost vertical cliffs of the escarpment before the partial descent to the plateau at Kijabe. Each of the cars were lowered in stages by a system of cogs and cables, like an elevator of sorts, nearly fifteen-hundred feet. The train then proceeded to Kijabe Station and down the remaining sixteen-hundred feet to the Rift Valley floor and onward to Molo. After they reached Molo, the Iron Rhino would continue on to Lake Victoria and Uganda. Gichuru would always remember this journey. It was an amazing bit of engineering!

Now, however, a new rail line had been built without the complex system of cogs and cables. Just before dawn, the three, Laikisat, Njage, and Gichuru alighted at Kijabe Station. They were excited about being able to have time to explore the land and the forest near Kijabe.

As the dawn broke, the vastness of the earth opened before them! First, they could see the enormous mound of the cratered Mt. Longonot rising from the Rift Valley floor below. They could almost touch it! On the eastern edge of the Valley in the far distance across the vast valley rose the shadow of the Mau Escarpment. It was spectacular!

As they started on foot walking up the hill as directed, they noticed a short, well-dressed *Mzungu* (European) man walking in the same direction with a young teenage man and a young African. What stood out was that the man had very large ears, which stuck out below the large brimmed hat. They assumed the boy was his son, and the African boy a servant. Gichuru could overhear the young *Mzungu* speaking quickly and rapidly in Gikuyu to the African! Gichuru had never heard a *Mzungu* speaking his language with such facility.

"Muriega!" he heard the Bwana call out to them as he turned to face Gichuru and the others. All three immediately looked amazed but returned the greeting.

The young teenager was first to reply in perfect Kikuyu. "I am called Hobeti, and this is my father. He is the head of our mission school at Kijabe. My friend is Johana."

"Ndimwega," replied Gichuru. "I am very impressed at your mastery of our difficult tongue."

"I was born here, and also my sister and brother. Where are you three headed? I see that your friend is a Maasai."

"Yes, Laikisat is a Maasai and has been fighting with Lord Delamare" protecting the border with Tanganyika. Njage here is a Meru who has also been in the war with the KAR near Kilimanjaro. They all are happy the war is ended and can now be back to normal life with their wives and children. We are headed to meet with a friend who has invited us to meet his clan."

"Muga, Njage. I believe that is the proper greeting in the Meru language, but I think you too can understand Gikuyu. Your languages are close," offered Hobeti.

"Mugamano! Yes," replied Njage. "You speak very well."

"Thank you."

Gichuru started to explain. "I attended a mission school at Kabete and have worked for the Government in Nairobi for quite a while. We are concerned about our lands and how life will change now. With the war ending and with the increase in settlement, we feel we are in more peril. The war, the drought, and the plague have caused much suffering for our people. We have also seen many swarms of locusts!"

Hobeti shook his head in understanding. "Yes, we too as missionaries are concerned. We want to help educate

Africans so that you can be as skilled and as prepared as the settlers. My father has been dedicated to education. He is a man of God but very educated and selfless.

"He and his wife first arrived even before the coming of the railroad. He paid children a penny a day to attend lessons to learn to read and write. He believed that these skills are needed, not only to understand the word of God, but also to compete in the modern world.

"My father also has set up saving accounts in the Nairobi bank for our workers, so they can save some money. Our mission is growing, and more missionaries are arriving each month."

Gichuru decided to tell Hobeti about himself. "Yes, we have been given opportunities under the British and at school. As I mentioned I attended the Scottish Mission School in Kabete. I have benefitted from my job as a clerk in Nairobi. I have had many opportunities. I have a fine family. I thank God.

"However, there are so many who struggle. Some have no land, or very small holdings. Wages are very low. There has been more suffering from the war, the influenza, and the drought. And most of all, we do not rule ourselves. We are not even being given a voice on the Legislative Council."

Njage spoke next. "And up country it is very bad, Hobeti. There are large plantations on our lands, but we do not receive compensation. Our people are forced to labor on the coffee estates to earn some money to help support their families, while we are allowed only small plots for ourselves to grow a few bananas, beans, and potatoes for subsistence. The drought has reduced our yield.

"Our men travel many miles from home and are separated from their wives and children for many months.

This leads to immorality and unwanted orphan children. Before the white man came, we had strict rules on warrior hood and marriage. It has all fallen away and we are left with problems."

Johana had been quiet for all this time. Finally, he spoke with authority. "I have been listening to you all. I understand what you are telling us. We have many of the same problems here at Kijabe. We are lucky to have this mission close to us and empathetic men like the Bwana who walks with us and treats us as equals. It is not the fault of one man or another. We all have our faults. It is the system of the world. The systems in the Congo and South Africa are much worse. We hear that our brothers there are treated more like slaves.

"I am still young, but I have had many opportunities here because of the Bwana, whom we affectionately call Bwana Big Ears. Hobeti and the others have also taught me much, especially about Christ and that there should be no master or slave. We are all equal and as you see, my friend here is just as Gikuyu as I am!

"As Hobeti said, his father paid me a penny a day to attend class when I was very young. He made me want to learn and I have been doing so ever since. I hope to become a minister to bring the Word of God to my people and help improve their earthly conditions.

"The African church is just below us on the edge of the plateau. The mission is very encouraging to us Africans. Someday we will have an African Church run by Africans."

The Bwana looked at the men with kind eyes. "I have seen much since arriving in East Africa. I came even before the Iron Rhino arrived here. My first home was in Kangundo. My wife and I arrived at Kijabe on ox carts.

Now, here in this place, truly an earthly paradise, I have also helped to found schools for educating both missionary children and Africans. The *Wazungu* children's parents are serving all over British East Africa teaching many different tribes. We hope Johana and people like him might someday be ministers to their own people. We call this place high above the Rift, '*A School in the Clouds!*'

Gichuru, shaking his head in affirmation, "E-e-e! These are noble goals. But, Bwana, how are we to be able to rule ourselves? Some of us are educated and our elders have ruled us wisely for ages. But now they have no power, and we must do as the British command. Even the Indians have begun to protest. *Mungu* (God) wishes us to be free. Is it not so?"

The Bwana noticed Gichuru's concern. He recognized the yearning that was in this man by the look in his eyes. He related their desire to his ancestors in the British America of long ago. "The time will come. There is a time for everything as the Bible says. You must be patient and pray. In our country we were ruled by the British for 150 years before we became independent."

"I did read your history at school. But you had to fight a bloody war lasting many years. I hope we can achieve freedom without bloodshed."

"We did fight a terrible war. I pray that men may have become more Christian and accepting since those days. Especially now since this Great War has caused so much suffering in the world. They call this War the *War to End all Wars*! Maybe men will learn. Self-rule will come."

"I hope so, but we become more impatient by the day."

Hobeti added, "Schooling is the way. Be patient, *marafiki* (friends). Now, where do you go from here?"

Gichuru continued, "Our friend has explained we take

this path upward toward the high forest."

On saying that, they looked up the hill and saw a man waving and running toward them."

"*Hamjambo!*" he yelled as he approached.

When he had descended, he greeted them all again and introduced himself.

"I am called Jomo, Jomo Kinyata. Pleased to meet you all. I have come to take my friends to our meeting and to show them the beauty of this place."

At this they all replied in unison as the four Africans started up the hill. "*Kwaheri!*"

"*Kwaheri!*"

With this they parted, the missionaries turning toward their school and the three Africans toward the forest, into their different worlds. One group fortified by faith and at least for now headed into the known; the other, into an unknown world filled with expectation, change, and danger. How each was to be affected by history was yet to be determined by forces beyond all their control. For now, each hoped that change would be peaceful. But each had a premonition that the world was changing rapidly since the end of the Great War and that things would not be this way for much longer.

In the forest the three heard many differing opinions and ideas about how Africans should organize and begin to lead their people. The one main idea that emerged is that they needed to proceed carefully. They did not want to lose other leaders like Harry Thuku because they knew the British had ways of discouraging protests. Also, other Africans who had benefited from helping the British were not interested in stirring the pot too violently.

All three had become wise in all they had seen over

these years. They had friends and colleagues from different tribes and even among the colonials and the missionaries. All had filled their heads with so much since the early days growing up in the mountains or plains.

The few years since the arrival of the Iron Rhino in Nairobi in 1900 to this meeting with Jomo in 1922 had moved them centuries in their minds. They now knew that the old ways were over, that there was good and bad in all men no matter what their label. The question was how best achieve freedom? Would it materialize as they all wanted and wished? Would there be pitfalls even when and if they gained it? Questions, questions, questions!

On the return from the forest to the Iron Rhino Station they had time to reflect and plan for the future. The three began to discuss what they had heard and seen. Gichuru was the first to philosophize.

"In the years since we were children our tribal ways were replaced by the *Wazungu*. They came like thieves in the night! Perhaps they did not intend to rob us. They saw what they thought was vacant land and settled on it. They did not realize it was our communal land where we took our cattle and goats when we needed it. They did not realize it was given to us by *Ngai* (God)! The Europeans arrived on the Iron Rhino and spread throughout our land. Like a thief in the night they came and took from us."

"Yes," replied Laikisat, "they took from us before we could realize what was gone!"

Then Njage added what he had seen in Meru. "First, they took our spears and arrows; then our ceremonies, our *Nkoma*, and our God. They sent us away from our wives and families and molded us to do their will. With their talk they disguised our collaboration by creating artificial positions of authority. We accepted because it seemed to increase our importance and help our families. We believed in them because we thought they had our well-being in mind! But it was all for controlling us!"

Laikisat was a man of few words, but of deep thought. He had been staring at the brightening sky in the east, as he listened to the others. Finally, he added, "*Marafiki* (friends), you see now why we Maasai are as we are. Why we cultivate fear in other tribes. Why we have refused so much that the white men wanted to put on us. You must learn from us!"

Gichuru thought for a while, then said, "Yes, *marafiki*, they are thieves, but now we understand. Now we have learned from them! But look at the horizon! Suddenly, the clear, cool African dawn is rising! It has opened our eyes to new possibilities. We shall persevere! We shall be victorious! This is what we have heard in our discussions with Jomo and the others! *'Harambee! Harambee! Tuimbe, pamoja!'* (Let's pull together! Sing together as one)!'"

So Laikisat bade his farewell and headed on foot down to the Rift Valley floor toward his *manyatta* (Maasai compound) on the plains south of Elmenteita, the great pink edged lake, north of the two great hills, Longonot and Suswa.

As Laikisat descended from the forest near Kijabe his heart became light. Finally, he was done with *Wazungu's* adventure. He would sit with the elders and he would tell them of his travels, and they would tell him of his history, of the journeys of his ancestors from the Nile. He would eat the roasted beef fixed by his wife and sit with his children.

His eldest son would soon be an *il-murran,* enter warrior hood. The circumcision date would be soon. But he would see that his son would go to a mission school. He must be better than Laikisat and learn the white man's alphabet. Some Africans had even been to Europe to a place called University. His son must also go so he could lead his people and learn the Wazungu's ways. He would need to help people like Gichuru and Kinyata. They must work together to gain independence and remain free. *Ngai* (God) will show him the way.

And as he descended and grew closer to his *manyatta* he felt the strong spirit of his grandfather, Laikisat, for whom he had been named, but had never known. He now felt Laikisat's spirit growing closer. His spirit had guided him through all his trials and had held him close on the night after his circumcision. He would be with him forever!

Njage accompanied Gichuru on the train to Nairobi. There Njage took his leave to purchase some supplies and begin the long journey to Meru. He would take the road north through the White Highlands. He would walk but try to ask for rides. He would sleep along the road. He had his large wool blanket which Horne had given him years ago. It would keep him warm, especially in the highlands near Timau.

He was looking forward to seeing his children again. His new place in Nkubu now seemed like home and far away from Mutindwa and District Officer. He would see that they too were educated to become ready for the new world. He would keep informed. Gichuru had promised to send him news. He would visit Gichuru. *Murungu* (God) had helped him so far, and the *Nkoma* (Spirits) would protect him.

And Gichuru, much older and wiser now, his work just beginning, arrived home to prepare for his journey. He was anxious, but excited about what had happened in the forest above Kijabe. Jomo had told him about the convention in London. Jomo needed an educated African to help him write, read, and prepare for the talks on Downing Street. Gichuru did not want to leave his family. He had left to go to Meru but had been home through the entire war. However, he realized what a great opportunity was opening for Africans. So, he had agreed. Great Britain! To London, the capital of the world! He might even see the Great King!

He would be helping Jomo begin a new era. Where would this lead? He had no idea. He was hopeful that progress would be made like that of the East Indians who would have representatives on the council. Would Africans be permitted? No, we need to demand! Gichuru and his children and all Africans must be treated as equals.

As Gichuru sat on his hill he felt very fortunate. This home was his and his children's. With his back against the forest on this perch he could look down over the growing city, non-existent when he was a child. It was early. The darkness was lifting. His mind reflected, *there are no masters and slaves!* He only hoped he and his children would see that day. Soon, soon. Soon he could see the sun! The African dawn! The cold and the darkness were lifting. Soon, soon, the magnificent light!

CHAPTER 37

POSTSCRIPT

In this fictional story I have tried as much as possible to remain consistent with historical facts and dates. When necessary for the story line, events may have taken place earlier or later than stated. Laikisat and Gichuru are made up characters, though Njage is an historical figure whom I have embellished. There is not much known about him besides his appointment as chief by Butler Horne. Butler Horne, Lord Delamare, Jomo Kenyatta (aka Kinyata) and the African Kaiser, among others, are historical figures. I have used some incidents in their lives, adding to them where necessary for interest.

I have tried to present East Africans of the late 19th and early 20th Centuries in a way true to their experiences. This was a very pivotal time in the colonization of this region where African, European, and Indian cultures intersected. The British stopped the slave trade but could be brutal colonizers. Missionaries brought education and western medicine but could be insensitive to African culture. Africans needed to be free and independent, but some old practices like circumcision were dangerous and brutal.

Since serving in Kenya in the U.S. Peace Corps in the 1970's, I have been fascinated with the interaction of different tribes and peoples. I believe the turn of the last century was pivotal in the formation of Kenya. East Africa would have to pass through three more decades of depression, war, and a nationalist Mau Mau uprising before independence was achieved. Today it is a thriving part of the world and a leading nation on the continent. Kenya has achieved a great deal in educating it populace and in bringing together diverse tribal cultures. Every profession both in Kenya and abroad, possesses distinguished Kenyan representatives. Though the country still suffers from political corruption, it is my hope that the good, intelligent, and gifted peoples of Kenya will come through this period and succeed in expanding freedom and prosperity.

List Of Tribes And Characters

BANTU

Gikuyu - south and west of Mt. Kenya
Kamba - east of Mt. Kenya to coast
Meru - north and east of Mt. Kenya
Swahili - coastal

NILOTIC

Maasai - on the plains in Great Rift Valley, northern Kenya, and south toward Mt. Kilimanjaro and into Tanzania

AFROASIATIC

Cushite-northern Kenya
Somali - northeastern Kenya and in what was previously Italian and British Somaliland

MINGEREZA — BRITISH

Sir William Mackinnon — Chairman Imperial British East Africa Company 1888-89

Sir Charles Elliot — Commissioner East African Protectorate 1900-1904

Sir Frederick John Jackson — Commissioner EAP 1904 and 1905

Sir James Hayes Sadler — Commissioner EPA 1905-09

Sir Edward Butler Horne — District Officer for Meru 1907-17

John B. Griffiths (Welsh) — Methodist Minister Embu and Meru 1906-7

Reverend Mimmack — Methodist Minister Nyeri and Meru 1909

Lord Delamere — Lord D — Influential Colonial

Mr. Weeks — Captain in charge of controlling Maasai

Note: I have used the term "Governor" liberally vs. Commissioner

WAJERUMANI — GERMANS

General Paul Von Lettow-Vorbeck — African Kaiser — Extraordinary German G

Family Trees

MAASAI-BURU CLAN

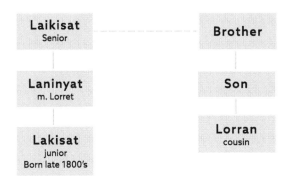

Laikisat
Senior

Brother

Laninyat
m. Lorret

Son

Lakisat
junior
Born late 1800's

Lorran
cousin

Letegall
Laikisat's boyhood friend

Koinet
one of Lord D's trusted Maasai

Mesobero
Maasai whose brother was murdered by Well's men
Loyal to Lord Delamere

GIKUYU

Kahara

Gichuru
m. Wanjiku
Born 1800's

Gothoro
Gikuyu Elder

Kamu Wa Ngengi
Jomo Kinyata
Revolutionary, Mau Mau Leader
First President of Kenya

Wahu
Kamau's first wife

MERU-LAWI CLAN

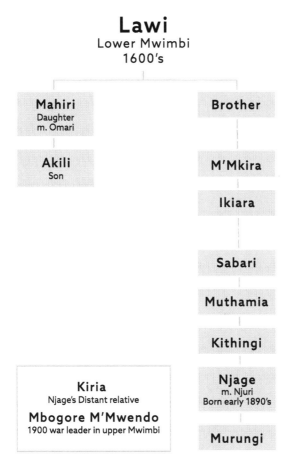

Lawi
Lower Mwimbi
1600's

Mahiri
Daughter
m. Omari

Brother

Akili
Son

M'Mkira

Ikiara

Sabari

Muthamia

Kithingi

Kiria
Njage's Distant relative

Mbogore M'Mwendo
1900 war leader in upper Mwimbi

Njage
m. Njuri
Born early 1890's

Murungi

SWAHILI-LAMU

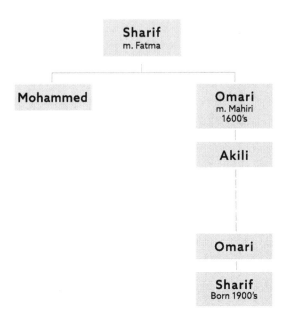

Sharif
m. Fatma

Mohammed

Omari
m. Mahiri
1600's

Akili

Omari

Sharif
Born 1900's

Timeline

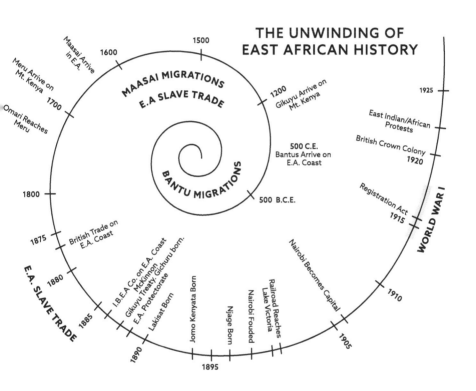

THE UNWINDING OF
EAST AFRICAN HISTORY

East Africa circa 1900

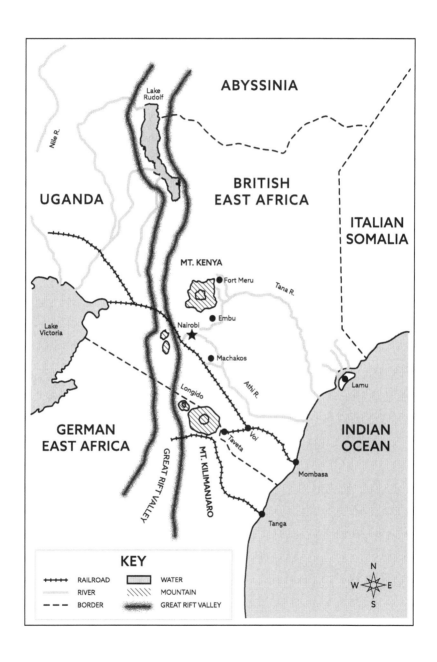

Great Rift Valley

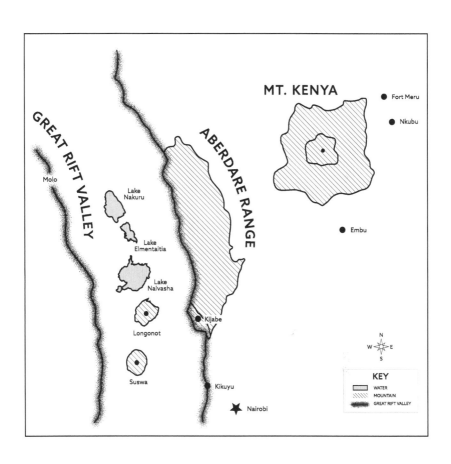

World War I Theater in East Africa

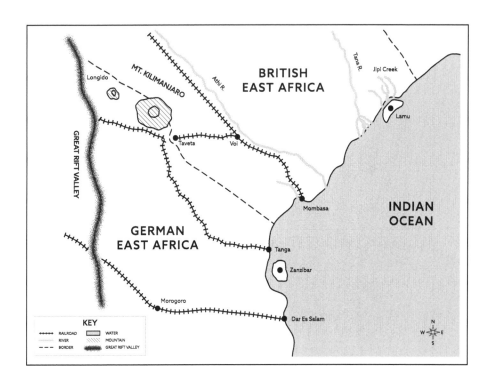

Bibliography

Books

Cranworth, Lord: *Kenya Chronicles*. London. Macmillan & Co. Ltd. 1939

Dinesen, Isak.: *Letters from Africa*. N.Y. USA. Viking Penguin. 1991

Fadiman, Jeffery A.: *When We Began There Were Witchmen, An Oral History From Mt. Kenya*. California, USA. U. of California Press. 1993

Farwell, Byron.: *The Great War in Africa* 1914-18. N.Y. London. WW. Norton & Co. 1989

Gaudi, Robert.: *African Kaiser*. N.Y. Dutton Caliber, Penguin Random House LLC. 2018

Huxley, Elsbeth.: *White Man's Country, V1,V2*. London. Chatto and Windus Ltd. 1980

Nine Faces of Kenya. N.Y. USA. Viking Penguin. 1991

Jackson, Sir Frederick.: *Early Days in East Africa*. London. Dawsons of Pall Mall. 1969

Miller, Charles.: *Lunatic Express*. Nairobi. Westlands Sundries Ltd. 1987

Mugane, John M.: *The Story of Swahili*. Ohio. Ohio U. Press. 2015

Articles and Websites

Barclay & Fry.: "British Colonial Reports. No. 791 East Africa Protectorate. 1912-13" London. His Majesties Stationary Office 1914 "No. 1153. Colony and Protectorate of Kenya - 1921." London.His Majesties Stationary Office. 1923

BBC.: "WWI: Kenya's Forgotten Heroes." 8/26/19 https://www.bbc.com/news/world_African_28836752

Crawfurd Homepage.: "Kenya Timeline" 8/12/19 https://crawfrud.dk/africa/kenya-timeline.html

Diop, Cheikh Anta.: "The Religion of the Maasai." 1/28/20. https://en.lisapoyakama.org

ERservicies. World. Civilizations.: "The Swahili Culture." 8/3/19 https://courses.lumenlearning.com/suny-hccc-worldcivilization/chapeter/the.swahili.culture.

Finke, Jens.: "Maasai - Religion and Beliefs." 12/11/19. https://bluegecko.org/kenya/tribes/maasai/beliefs.htm

Finke's, Jens.: "Meru Religion and Beliefs." 12/29/19 https://bluegecko.
org/Kenya/tribes/meru/beliefs.htm.

Kenya information guide. "The Mijikenda Tribe." 5/2/20. https://www.
Kenya-information-guide-com/mijikenda-tribe-html

Nation Media Group.: " The Origin of Nairobi City." 8/12/19. https://
nation.co.ke/counties/ nairobi/The-origin-of-nairobi-city/1954174-
1950392-130n5dh/index.html

Taruis, Isaac Kipsang.: "A History of the Direct Taxation of the African
People of Kenya 1895-1973." Rhodes U. 2004. British Archives

The Ameru. "The Ameru." 12/29/19. https://www.Ameru.co.ke/death-in-
ancient.meru/

U. Of Pennsylvania: "East Africa Living Encyclopedia- Kenya History."
8/3/19 https://www.africa.upenn.edu/NEH/khistory.htm

Wikipedia.: "Maasai People." 1/28/20 https://en.wikipedia.org/wiki/
maasai-people

Wikipedia.: "Commissioners and Governors of East Africa." 8/13/19.
https://en.wikipedia.org/wiki/list-of-colonial-governors.and.
administrators.of.Kenya

Wikipedia.: "Meru." 8/256/19 https://en.wikipedia.org/wiki/Meru-Kenya.

Wikipedia.: "Henry Kitchener, 2nd Earl Kitchener." 4/27/20. https://
en.wikipedia.org/wiki/Henry_Kitchener,_2nd_Earl_Kitchener

Wikipedia.: "Hugh Cholmondeley, 3rd Baron Delamare. 8/18/19
https://en.wikipedia.org/wiki/Hugh_Cholmondeley,_3rd_Baron_
Delamare_#African_expeditionary_explorer

Wikipedia.: "East African Campaign WWI." 9/22/19. https://
en.wikipedia.org/wiki/East.African.Campaign.(World.War.I.)

Wikipedia.: "Battle of Kilimanjaro." 9/23/19. https://en.wikipedia.org/
wiki/Battle.of.Kilimanjaro.

Wikipedia.: "History of Nairobi." 4/22/20 https://enwikipedia.org/wiki/
History-of-Nairobi

Wikipedia.: "Jomo Kenyatta." 9/18/19. https://en.wikipedia.org/wiki/
Jomo_Kenyatta.

Wikipedia.: "East African Campaign." 8/26/19. https://en.wikipedia.org/
wiki/East_African_campaign(world_war_I)

Wilson, Sally: "Battler of Longido." 9/23/19. https://pomathorn.
pressbooks.com/chapter/battle.of.longido.west?

Zelaza, Tiyambe, et.al.: "Colonialism in Kenya: Kikuyu Organizing
against the British." 9/17/19 Source watch.org.

Endnotes

1. en.m.wikipedia.org/wikii/List_of_colonial_governors_and_administrators_of_ Kenya;pg2

2. Wikipedia: History of Nairobi, en.wikipedia.org/wiki/History_of_Nairobi

3. A History of Direct Taxation of the African Peoples of Kenya, 1895-1973; Isaac Kipsang Tarus; Pg 60

4. African Studies Center and Wikipedia

5. When We Began There Were Witchmen by Jeffery A. Fadiman Pg 131-134ff

6. When We Began There Were Witchman

7. White Man's Country, V 1, Elsbeth Huxley, Pg 57

8. When We Began There Were Witchmen. Pg 134 ff

9. When We Began, There Were Witchman. Pg. 207

10. African Kaiser by Robert Gaudi, pg 119 ff

11. Wikipedia: James Hayes Sadler (colonial administrator): en.wikipedia/wiki/ James_Hayes_Sadler_(colonial_administrator) pg 1

12. The term given to the Kenyan train by Charles Miller in his 1971 book by that name.

13. African Kaiser; Robert Gaudi; pg 34. Educated in guerrilla tactics at Kassel; Gross-Lichterfelde.

14. White Man's Country; Elsbeth Huxley; Chapter XIV

15. cdc.gov: 1918 Pandemic (H1N1 virus) page 1

16. Nine Faces of Kenya; Elspeth Huxley; pg 141

17. White Man's Country; V 2; Pg 39-49 Elsbeth Huxley

18. East African Campaign; wikipedia.org/EastAfridancampaign.WorldWarI

19. Catha Edulis, Myrrh grown in Meru District.

20. White Man's Country; Vol 2; Elsbeth Huxley; pg 116. Colonial Report 1153;Colony and Protectorate of Kenya1921; pg6-7

21. White Man's Country; Vol2; Elsbeth Huxley; pg 121 and ChapterXVIII

22. White Man's Country;Vol 2; Elsbeth Huxley; Pg 123

23. White Man's Country; Vol 2; Elsbeth Huxley; pg 140 and Ch XIX

24. wikipedia.org/wiki/Jomo_Kenyatta;Pg6

25. wikipedia.org/wiki/Jomo_Kenyatta;pg6

Printed in Great Britain
by Amazon